# DEATH BY ASSOCIATION 2

# ERNEST MORRIS

GOOD 2 GO PUBLISHING

**DEATH BY ASSOCIATION 2**

Written by Ernest Morris
Cover Design: Davida Baldwin, Odd Ball Designs
Typesetter: Mychea
ISBN: 978-1-947340-58-9
Copyright © 2020 Good2Go Publishing
Published 2020 by Good2Go Publishing
7311 W. Glass Lane • Laveen, AZ 85339
www.good2gopublishing.com
https://twitter.com/good2gobooks
G2G@good2gopublishing.com
www.facebook.com/good2gopublishing
www.instagram.com/good2gopublishing

# PROLOGUE

RICKY PUT THE GLASS TUBE TO HIS LIPS, STRUCK THE lighter, and inhaled the crack into his lungs. He then passed the tube and lighter to Pretty Boy. Not in a million years would Mack have thought his right-hand man would turn into a crackhead.

"This is that fire that Mack got," Ricky said as he exhaled the crack smoke.

As Pretty Boy exhaled the crack smoke, his ears popped. The high hit him instantly.

"Damn, this shit is good. I'ma need some of this for the block. What's the prices on this shit?"

Ricky's jaw was locked as he tried to respond. "Woo woo, one twenty-five a ba, ba, ball, and eight an ounce."

"Damn, that's cheap. I'ma need an ounce," Pretty Boy said.

Ricky continued to fill the glass tube. Rock after rock. He didn't realize how much the two had smoked. It was three in the morning and the high was calm. Ricky questioned Pretty Boy about Zeus.

"What's up with Zeus? I haven't seen him since I got shot. He's been ducking me."

"Nah, Ricky. It's not like that. Zeus been fucked up. A few weeks ago the stash spot got hit. So he's been running around trying to make money."

"What? Who got him? Why nobody told me? What they get?"

"They got him for all that work from the Easton nigga. Shit put a dent in his pockets."

In life, Karma's a muthafucka, and Ricky didn't even think of it. They continued to speak on the robbery and how shit didn't fall into place. Then there was a knock on the door. When Ricky answered it, it was some lady that lived down the street from them. She was wearing a skimpy skirt and tank top. She smelled the crack and wanted some. Since she didn't have any money, they had other things in mind. When she came in and sat down, Ricky and Pretty Boy could see that she wasn't wearing panties. They passed her the tube and lighter.

"Hit this shit, so we can hit that pussy."

She took a couple of pulls, and her eyes closed as she leaned back on the bed. She was feeling the effects already. Pretty Boy was the first to get closer to her. He lifted her already short skirt up to her waist, exposing her clean-shaved pussy. Both of them instantly bricked up.

"Come on, because I have to get back home before my husband gets off of work," she said, opening her legs wider for them to get a better view of her goodies.

Ricky walked over to where her face was, while Pretty Boy started eating her pussy. She took Ricky's dick into her mouth, and the warmness almost had him cumming immediately. Pretty Boy could smell a pissy scent coming from her vagina, but he didn't care about it. All he wanted to do was fuck the beautiful lady. After a couple of minutes of licking the pussy, he pulled down his pants and entered her raw. He didn't even think about wearing a condom.

"Damn, you gotta get some of this. Her shit is fire, Ricky," Pretty Boy said as he continued pumping away. He was on the verge of busting a nut. "How's her head game?"

Ricky's eyes were closed as he enjoyed the warmness of her tongue working its magic around the tip of his dick. "This shit is off the chain, bro."

Pretty Boy lifted her legs up to his shoulders so he could really kill it. He was trying his best to make his dick touch her stomach.

"Please, I can't stand it, baby. I'm begging you. Please hurry up and cum," she panted as she stopped sucking Ricky's dick to talk to Pretty Boy.

Her screams were washed away by her moaning and groaning, just as he knew they would be each time he filled her up with all ten inches. Each stroke was slow and sensual. It didn't take either one of them long to reach the climax they had been anticipating. He came inside her.

Once he was done, they switched positions. Ricky did the same thing and entered her without a condom. If it wasn't for the crack, they probably would have been thinking.

"Oh my God, you're so big," she moaned, feeling her walls being stretched as he pumped in and out of her. He didn't last more than two minutes before he also shot his load inside her.

Once they were done with the woman, she got up off the bed and left. Pretty Boy did the same, but not before they had another hit of the crack. Ricky was so high that he fell asleep right in the bed that all of their semen was on. He didn't care.

With a few hours of sleep, Ricky showered up, got dressed, and headed to the Gardens. It was collection day. Every Sunday, Mack would collect the week's earnings. Ricky knew that he would be in the doghouse after smoking almost an ounce of crack with Pretty Boy and the lady from down the street.

Five o'clock came quickly. Ricky collected from each of his runners—$3,000 apiece off four $1,000 packs. If they took no shorts, the runners would have easily pocketed a stack, so everybody ate. Even after smoking the twenty-one grams, Ricky's count was still correct. He still had work from the quarter brick that Mack gave him. One hundred and sixty grams had been chopped up for the runners.

Ninety had been left for Ricky. He smoked twenty-one, which left him with almost seventy grams to play with. He was to report twelve thousand, five hundred dollars back to Juice for Mack. He got twelve stacks. He was in debt for five hundred. It didn't seem like much to a hustler, but it's all about stacking in the game. All Ricky wanted to do was get high and smoke all his profit. He did all his collections, then left to the south side.

~ ~ ~

"You collected everything from everyone?" Mack asked Juice as he smoked.

"I seen Vic and Husky. They peeled me the twelve five for the work, and eight for the bud. Off the eight, I gave them back twenty-five hundred and told them to split it down the middle."

"What about Ricky?"

"I still haven't collected anything from him yet. He was out there collecting, and then he disappeared. I got ten from my spot and five from the weed. Have you heard from him?"

"Nah, I haven't seen him since the party. I've been hanging with Erica. She's a handful. But I'll get up with him. In the meantime, how's things with Fat Freddy?"

"He's been feeling the pressure. I guess he thinks that we will eventually run out and then he'll be back on top again. He still have his loyal customers," Juice said.

"Good. As long as everyone is eating. Is everybody out?"

"Rob and I are. Vic and Husky should be almost out. I'll check on that."

"Aight. I'ma head out, grab some more work, then make a move. I'll be back in a couple hours. I'll stop by Ricky's too." Mack gave Juice a pound and hopped in his car. "I hope Ricky didn't fuck up the money," he said out loud.

He knew that Ricky wouldn't betray him, but he wasn't dealing with Ricky anymore. He was now dealing with Ricky on crack, and the crack will make a fiend turn on his own mother if she gets in the way of him getting high. Mack's mind was going in circles as he headed across town. His mind was on the $12,000 Ricky had. He placed his system on five, so he could barely hear his subwoofers thump.

Riding with $33,000, tinted windows, through the middle of the city at seven at night was an easy target for the cops. He hit every alley until he reached Ricky's house. As Mack pulled up, he noticed a black Expedition with four dudes inside, sitting four houses away from Ricky's house. He slowly drove past the SUV without stopping. He took a glance inside the SUV's window, trying to see a face. The driver had a fitted cap that lay low over his eyes, which made it hard for him to recognize the person. He noticed something else that caught his eye. It was the bright orange H that sat on the fitted cap.

Houston Astros hats are known to be worn by members of the Hole. Mack was confused. Was Zeus plotting on Ricky, or was they waiting on him? He circled the block and parked six cars behind the black SUV. After ten minutes of surveillance, the black SUV pulled out of the parking space, without anyone getting in.

Forgetting about the $33,000 that was in his possession, he pulled out and followed the SUV. It headed toward Big Poppa's spot. Mack was so caught up with following the SUV that he didn't notice the Chevy Astro that had pulled up beside him. It was too late. All Mack heard was the shots in the air.

POP! POP! POP! POP! POP! POP! POP! POP! POP! POP!

Mack's car was riddled with bullets. He stepped on the gas pedal. More shots rang out, hitting his vehicle three more times. He swerved his car side to side like a slithering snake as he dodged the bullets and played chicken with the traffic.

Mack felt hot liquid coming down his face. The first thing he thought was that he was shot, but he didn't know where. His face was leaking, but it wasn't enough for him to stop. He was still conscious, and his adrenaline was pumping. He was mad because he was caught off guard once again.

Blood covered his eyes as he wiped them in order to see. He pulled into an empty parking spot outside his house. Face bloody, he popped the trunk and grabbed the money. He looked at his riddled car. It was a wonder that he wasn't dead right now. Mack jogged to his house, touching his body making sure he didn't have any bullet holes. He opened the door and slammed it shut behind him.

"Mack, what happened to you?" Lo yelled as he watched Mack take a couple more steps before falling to the floor in a puddle of blood.

# ONE

"ONE THOUSAND, TWO, THREE, FOUR, FIVE, SIX, SEVEN, eight, nine, ten, eleven, twelve thousand. It's all here," Ricky said to himself as he inhaled the laced dutch. "Now it's time to celebrate," he said out loud while he stashed the money in a shoebox and placed it in the closet.

Ricky threw on his sneaks and a T-shirt. Zeus was throwing a get-together for a bunch of his men, and he planned to invite some strippers. Ricky had been calling and texting Mack for the past twelve hours to pay off his tab, but he didn't respond back. The two brothers hadn't spoken in two weeks. He was busy running around pushing nickels and dimes to get all of Mack's money and extra for his profit. After there was no response from Mack, Ricky called Pretty Boy.

"Ricky, what's good?" Pretty Boy asked when he answered his cell.

"Just got ready. What's the address?"

"2614 Snowflake Drive. Room 101, at the Econo Lodge, right off of Lehigh Street."

"Aight bet," Ricky said as he wrote the address and

room number down on a piece of paper. "I'ma call this Uber and make my way toward you in a few."

"Bet," he replied before ending the call.

A half hour later, Ricky pulled up to the hotel. The Uber parked in front of room 101. He peeled off a twenty-dollar bill and passed it to the driver and told him to keep the change. As he approached the door, he could hear loud music playing inside. He knocked on the door and waited for someone to answer. Seconds later, an Asian stripper opened the door topless, with only a thong on.

"You must be Ricky," she said seductively. "We've been waiting for you."

Ricky's dick got excited instantly as the stripper grabbed his hand and pulled him inside the hotel room, then threw him on the bed. She straddled his body, while the other stripper that was on top of Pretty Boy cheered them on. "Put it on her," Pretty Boy said, hyping Ricky up.

Zeus was caught up in the bathroom with two strippers, one Brazilian and the other Armenian, while Big Poppa had two twins. The white American twins played no games. Big Poppa sat on the love seat as one twin sat on his lap grinding on his dick, while the sister grinded her pussy on his face. Pretty Boy was laid up on the full-size bed with an exotic Spanish stripper now in the sixty-nine position. The hotel room smelled of expensive perfume and pussy.

The party was jumping from the minute Ricky stepped foot in the room. The Asian stripper teased Ricky as he lay flat on the bed. Next thing he knew, his shorts came off and the stripper had his dick in her mouth with his boxers still on. He was infatuated with the freaky shit going on. The last time he had sex with an Asian was when he went to a massage parlor out 309. After a quick tease the stripper pulled off his boxers and went to work, slipping the condom on his dick. She slowly straddled his torso and lowered her pussy on his hardness. She gave out a sexy moan. The entire hotel room was in an all-out orgy.

Pretty Boy had the Spanish stripper held in the air while he thrust into her pussy. Big Poppa was sucking one of the twin's pussy while her sister rode his dick. Ricky switched position on the Asian girl and was now hitting her doggy style. She was yelling in her language as he continued to pound her from behind.

"I'm cumming, I'm cumming," she yelled, letting her juices flow freely from her pussy.

Once Pretty Boy put down the Spanish stripper, she immediately went over to Ricky, wanting a piece of his dick.

"Hey, papi. Want some of this carne?" she asked, grabbing her fat ass.

Ricky slipped out of the Asian girl's pussy and reached for the Latina. He put her in the doggy-style position. He looked at her ass in amazement as he slid inside her hot walls. Her pussy was tight and wet. She began moaning uncontrollably. The Asian chick went over to Big Poppa, and the twins went to Pretty Boy. Zeus was out of sight. He was keeping his exotic strippers to himself as he fucked them in the shower and Jacuzzi. The entire night was crazy for all of them. They got to fuck four badass strippers.

After three hours of straight fucking and sucking, the girls went right to sleep. Zeus gathered up his crew, and they went into the adjoining room so they could talk business. As soon as they were all settled, Zeus spoke up first.

"Ricky, I'm glad that you could make it. How's the wounds?"

This was the first time Ricky and Zeus had seen each

other since the robbery. "They good. I'm better now, but where have you been?" Ricky asked.

"I've been running around all crazy trying to recoup all the money I lost. I got hit a couple of weeks ago."

"Yeah, I heard about that. Pretty Boy told me."

"Any suspects?" Zeus asked. "'Cause that muthafucka won't make it past the night."

"Nah, nothing."

"Well we ain't here for that," Zeus spoke up. "I got this Dominican cat that we gonna meet tomorrow. He's bringing us five kilos to check out. We all gotta be on our best behavior. I ain't trying to mess this thing up."

In Ricky's mind, he felt a different vibe. Zeus had manipulated them into a sex party, then brought up an unexpected meeting with a plug. Last time Zeus came up with a plan, Ricky ended up shot twice as a result of it. He was paranoid, but not stupid. So he plotted something in his head.

"What time is he sliding through tomorrow?" Ricky asked.

"Ten thirty sharp," Zeus responded.

"Aight, I'ma call me an Uber. I have something I need

to take care of. I'll be back in a few hours."

Zeus wasn't sure why Ricky wanted to bail, so he offered a ride, and he accepted. He didn't want to look suspicious. As they drove off, Ricky told Zeus to stop at his moms so he could pick up his gun. Zeus was surprised he wasn't strapped. "You slipping, young boy."

"Nah, I was just excited about the strippers. Plus, I'm in good hands with you, right?" Ricky said subliminally as he gave Zeus a funny look.

Zeus laughed at his excuse for getting caught slipping. He pulled up to Ricky's spot without even verifying the location. Ricky never showed anybody where he rested except Mack and Pretty Boy, but Pretty Boy only entered through the rear. Ricky wasn't slipping on this one. He hopped out of the Suburban and walked to the back of his house. Along the walk, he called Mack's phone but got no answer. He then texted him with the emergency code. Fifteen minutes went by, and still no answer from him.

"Damn, he must be mad over the money." Ricky grabbed his Desert Eagle and headed back to the SUV. "My bad I took so long," he told Zeus when he got back in the car.

~ ~ ~

At ten thirty sharp, a knock came to the hotel door. Zeus gave everyone the get on point look. Ricky grabbed his gun and headed toward the attached room. Pretty Boy, Big Poppa, and Zeus stood in room 101. As soon as Zeus opened the door, he was greeted with a chrome 45 to his face. The entire room got quiet; no one said a word. All you heard was the air conditioner running.

"You know why I'm here," Rico said.

Zeus had no idea that the Dominican dude was part of Rico's organization. He was shocked when Rico entered the room like a boss after his bodyguards walked Zeus down.

"No, I don't," yelled Zeus. "Now tell your goons to get their fucking guns out my face."

Rico said nothing. He jumped on the phone and told the person on the other end to come in. Two seconds later another man walked through the door.

"Do you remember Johnny?" Before Zeus could answer, Rico cut him off. "You were dealing with him a couple of months ago. Around the same time, he was robbed. Do you know anything about that?"

"I don't know what you're talking about."

"Okay. So do you have the hundred grand for the kilos?"

Zeus hesitated before he answered. He knew he didn't have it. "I, I, I was trying to see the work first, and if it's official, I was going to get the money."

Rico was far from an idiot. He sensed Zeus was lying. He gave one of his shooters a look, and he shot Zeus in the leg. There was no sound. The shooter had a silencer on his weapon. Zeus dropped to the ground holding his wounded leg as Pretty Boy and Big Poppa stood frozen like Popsicles.

"So you were planning on robbing me again?" Rico asked.

"Nah, we wasn't planning to rob you. None of us have guns on us. I told you we wanted to make sure everything was straight first. I just got robbed, and I didn't want to get robbed again," Zeus tried to explain, begging for his life as blood seeped out of his leg.

While Zeus was being held at gunpoint in room 101, Ricky in 102 managed to escape and was plotting on the Dominican connect. Ricky was confused about why a man exited and continued his surveillance waiting for the right time to strike.

"Where's your little punk ass friend Ricky at? Is he

hiding in the room attached to this one?" Rico asked with a sinister smile.

Zeus began to sweat. He knew that he was a dead man. He knew that Ricky was posted up in the attached room with his burner. "It's empty."

The bodyguard entered the other room with his gun aimed at the ready position. After a thorough search of the room, he returned to where the others were. "It's empty."

As sweat dripped off of Zeus's forehead, he felt a sense of relief, but deep down inside he felt that Ricky had bailed on him and the rest of the crew. What Zeus didn't know was that Ricky was outside plotting to rob the connect when he came out. Rico knelt down beside Zeus and tapped his face a couple of times.

"Today's your lucky day. I ain't going to kill you and your team for robbing me."

"I, I."

"Shut up!" yelled Rico. "You bring me Ricky, and I'll forget about the kilo and twenty thousand that you took from me. But if you don't deliver him to me, I will kill you and everyone you love, starting with your fat-ass nephew." He looked at Big Poppa. "TWO WEEKS! Am I fucking clear?"

"Yes, I'll bring you Ricky," Zeus replied in pain.

Big Poppa and Pretty Boy were frozen solid. They nearly pissed themselves as they watched Rico and his crew leave the hotel room. Between two parked cars, Ricky noticed the door opening to the room where Zeus and the others were. As soon as he was about to make his move, he noticed Rico exiting with his goons and two other men. He identified one as the dude Mack robbed, and the others he wasn't sure about. He was confused. His mind was spinning, wondering why they were there. Without going back to the hotel, Ricky managed to escape unseen.

# TWO

"HOW MUCH IS THAT JEEP RIGHT THERE?"

"That Jeep is $10,000."

"Does it come fully loaded with rims?"

"No, but we can arrange something if you like."

"Aight. You put some shoes on her and we have a deal."

"How would you like to pay? Cash, credit, or the obvious, finance."

"Don't disrespect me in front of my lady," Mack said, giving the salesman a cold stare. "Everything straight cash with me."

After he had called Princess and explained the shootings, she quickly drove to Allentown and brought him back to New York. She pampered her man's cut-up face like he was one of her patients. Mack's car was hit seven times. Three hit his driver's-side door, and one bullet shattered his window nearly hitting him in the face. The shattered glass ripped through his flesh, leaving him with a few gash marks.

During the stay, Princess showed him around her city, but she could tell that he was focused on his business. Every ten minutes he looked at his phone checking for any missed calls. Before he had left, he handed Juice two bricks cooked up and the rest of the weed he had left.

Princess tried her hardest to keep Mack's mind in NY, but it wasn't working. She took him to one of the finest restaurants, called The Diamond Princess in Manhattan. Then she took him to the best barbershop, called Elegant Kutz, where celebrities would frequently visit to get their cuts. She also had him meet with her parents for dinner. They instantly fell in love with him, especially her father. Mack was really starting to feel Princess and her family. They were perfect, and she was perfect in his eyes.

Mack wasn't sure if he was ready to settle down and deal with the long-distance relationship. During their drive back to Allentown, he thought very hard about his future. So to relieve all the stress he was feeling, he decided to go car shopping. Mack placed ten grand on top of the salesman's desk. His eyes opened wide at the sight of all that cash sitting there. He was surprised to see a young man with all that money. Princess quickly grabbed the money off the desk. She was hiding a secret from Mack and her close friends. She never mentioned a word to anybody as to who her father had become. No one questioned her, and in Mack's mind her father was just a businessman. The truth was Princess's father was one of the biggest kingpins in the Bronx, Carlos "Carlito" Pagan. He had gotten out of the game a year before his Columbian connect went down and got indicted by the US government. The reason for his departure, he was almost gunned down by his rival enemies, the Mexican Cartel. During the ten-year run, he made over $50 million. Her father owned three five-star restaurants in Manhattan and two barbershops, one in the Bronx and the other in Queens. She was rich and knew all about the drug game. Princess placed the money in her Gucci bag and pulled out her matching purse. "Sorry, pa, nothing over nine stacks. The feds will investigate, plus you just got your license. Where are you going to say you got the money from? Here, just put it on this." She pulled out a credit card and placed it on the desk.

Mack was surprised. He didn't know Princess knew all about the drug game and the alphabet boys. "You got a lot of explaining to do."

She filled out the paperwork and placed the Jeep under Mack's name as a gift. After they exited the dealership, Princess followed Mack to his house. Mack parked the

Jeep and hopped in her Lexus.

"So are you going to explain to me about that card you pulled out?"

"Do I have to?" she asked.

"Yes, you do. I feel like you're hiding something."

"Nah, pa, I ain't hiding anything from you. I just don't like to tell people 'bout my family."

"What about your family? See, there is something that you're not telling me."

"When you met my father, he told you about the businesses he owns. But he didn't mention to you how he inherited the money." Mack gave her his full attention as she continued. "Well I didn't want you to like me because my family has money. I wanted you to like me for me."

"I love you for you, Princess, with or without money." That was the first time Mack had ever told another woman other than his mother, grandmother, and sister that he loved them.

Princess's insides started to quiver. She was excited that Mack was the first to express his love. She also loved him, so she began to tell him her secret. "My father was one of New York's biggest kingpins. He managed to escape the prison cells. He was almost gunned down by the Mexican Cartel. Once he got shot he decided that the game was over. The restaurant we went to, Diamond Princess, is owned by him. He named it after my sister and I, and he also owns Elegant Kutz. Mack thought to himself. He never even realized that the bill was never paid at dinner, nor did the waitress give them a receipt. Then he thought how the barbers were all friendly and gave him a sample cut for his first haircut outside of PA. It was all because of his girlfriend's ties. She continued, "Growing up as the boss's daughter, I listened a lot, and my father taught me valuable lessons. One thing I learned is you can't spend over $9,000 unless you have a paper trail to cover that expense. The IRS will be knocking at your front and back door." Mack's dick got hard listening to Princess schooling him. She was right about everything she was saying. "I almost got caught slipping when . . ."

Mack leaned in, cutting her words off, and gently planted a kiss on his beautiful girlfriend's soft lips.

"Thank you, babe. I am truly grateful for you, and to have you in my life. Now since you have ten grand in your pockets, I assume dinner is on you tonight."

"I think I can manage that."

Princess stopped at one of her favorite restaurants, Red Lobster. They had a marvelous dinner. They both opened up to each other. This time she told him everything she witnessed. When the night was over, Mack invited Princess to spend the night, instead of driving back to New York. She accepted his offer. He gave her a pair of his boxers and a white tee to sleep in. Princess cuddled into his arms and fell asleep. Mack watched her sleep peacefully for an hour before he dozed off himself.

~ ~ ~

"Mack, are you there?" Lo screamed as he barged into his room. His eyes opened wide when he saw the beautiful woman in his brother's bed. "Ooops, my fault." He quickly closed the door.

"Lo, what's up? Come in. It's cool."

Lo opened the door again, this time slowly. He walked in with his head to the ground, embarrassed that he had busted in on them a couple of seconds ago. "Nothing, I wanted to give you this bag that Ricky dropped off a couple of days ago. He said that he's been calling you and you haven't picked up. I told him about the shooting, and he was pissed that no one told him that you had gotten shot at." Lo couldn't take his eyes off of Princess, and suddenly his mouth spoke without thinking. "Damn, she's fine." He put his hand over his mouth, embarrassed yet again.

Mack and Princess started to laugh. "You crazy, bro. Put the bag on the dresser."

After Lo sat the bag down, Mack introduced Lo to his girl. "Princess, that's my lil brother Lo. Lo, this fine woman that you see is the new member in my life, Princess."

"He's cute with those blue eyes," Princess shot back, getting Lo to blush.

"Watch her, Mack." Lo was quick on the draw also. They all shared another laugh, and then Lo headed back out the door. Before he closed it, he turned around and took one last look at Princess. Her beauty was as natural as it could get for a woman.

Mack finally got up and took a shower. When he stepped back into the room, he was wearing nothing but a towel wrapped around his waist. Princess admired his chiseled chest. She had plans for him, though. Each time they had slept together, he never once tried to make a move on her. That was only making her want him more. He was a complete gentleman, and today she was going to reward him. Princess hopped from under the sheets with only a thong on. Mack's eyes widened like a deer caught in the headlights. She pushed him down on the bed and straddled him. She then whispered in his ear. "You deserve all of me, babe. Take me into your world."

An hour later, they were getting out of the shower from exploring each other's bodies. Mack got dressed and tossed Princess another pair of boxers, a white tee, and a pair of sweatpants. "Here, put this on and let's go shopping."

"Okay," she replied, putting on the clothes.

~ ~ ~

After two hours of shopping, Mack parked at Jessica's crib. He walked Princess to the door, gave her a kiss, and then headed to the block. He was greeted by Vic, Juice, and Junito.

"Damn, cuz, where have you been? We've been trying to contact you for days," Juice stated.

"I was laid up with Princess. She introduced me to her fam. Did you find out who tried to kill me?" You could see the flames in Junito's eyes when Mack asked that question. He was sick that he wasn't there to protect him. Junito walked away from the conversation because he felt like he let Mack down.

"Word is that the nigga Zeus had something to do with it," Juice said.

"Oh yeah. That's what I was thinking. I haven't heard from Ricky, but he dropped off the tab to Lo," Mack told them.

"Well Ricky was up here the other day. He explained to us that he was at some stripper party with Zeus, then they were supposed to meet a plug."

"Oh yeah," Mack said, interested in what else he had to say. "Yeah, but the plug happened to be down wit Rico. Ricky said that he thinks Zeus was trying to set main man up. He tried to get in touch with you, but you never returned his calls or text messages."

Mack stood quiet absorbing the information. "You think that Diesel told Zeus that we robbed him?"

"Nah, I doubt it. Either way, Zeus tried to kill me. He's a mark."

Just as they were talking, an all-black Chevy Blazer pulled up. The windows were tinted, but the passenger window was rolled down. Gunshots erupted. POP! POP! POP! POP! POP! POP! The sounds of a TEC ripped through the south side. Mack, Juice, and Vic jumped behind a parked car. Bullets were heard hitting the car's metal frame. Then a second gun went off. BOOM! BOOM! BOOM! Mack noticed Junito exit from behind one of the project row homes, into the street, letting off three shots from his .357. The shots went straight through the front windshield. Then there was another round of shots flying. The Blazer swerved out of control, sideswiping two parked cars before making a right out of the Gardens. Junito ran toward the woods as Mack, Vic, and Juice got off the ground and ran toward Jessica's.

~ ~ ~

Mack sat on his mother's sofa staring at the black TV. He was furious. In broad daylight someone had the balls to go to the projects and light shit up. Princess was worried because he hadn't said a word in an hour. He could see the worried look on her face. "I'm okay, baby. Just thinking about who could be out there trying to kill me."

"Who would want to harm you?" He didn't want to tell her everything, but he knew she was definitely a ride-or-die chick.

"Ma, before I met you, Ricky and I were running with this guy name Zeus. He put us on to a robbery. The guy we robbed was affiliated with a kingpin named Rico."

"Do they know that you're the one who robbed them?" Princess asked, interrupting him.

"No, no one knows, just Zeus, Ricky, and now you. Then Ricky went on another robbery with Zeus. Shit went bad, and Ricky got shot. I felt like Zeus set him up, so I got the drop on Zeus stash house and robbed him."

"So, you think Zeus or Rico is out to get you?"

"I don't know. I'm trying to figure it out, but that's not all."

"Go head babe, I'm listening."

"Then Ricky goes and robs Rico at his barbershop."

"What? The kingpin again? Is he fucking crazy?"

Through all the madness, Mack had forgotten that Ricky had left him a message. After explaining to his girl all his dirt, he remembered the money. Mack went to his room, opened the bag, and read the note. He grabbed his keys and gave them to Princess, then told her to drive him to Ricky's.

Mack spoke to Ricky. Ricky explained to him about the night and morning at the hotel. The duo put their minds together and decided that Zeus and Rico were their prime suspects, but they couldn't jump the gun. They wanted to wait until they were 100 percent sure who was behind all the shootings. Mack had a plan to test the waters.

# THREE

"LO! LO!" LO HEARD HIS NAME BEING CALLED FROM ACROSS the park. From afar he could see Kim waving her hand, motioning him to come to her house.

"I wonder what the hell she wants," Lo said out loud, walking toward her house. As he got closer, he could see that she had her cell phone to her ear.

"Here, someone wants to talk to you."

"For me?" Lo asked. He was confused as he grabbed the phone and put it to his ear.

"Hello!" a familiar voice came through the phone that quickly put a smile on his face.

"Hey, Jazzy. Where are you at? Are you home?" Lo had a million questions for her and decided to ask them all at once.

"One question at a time," Jazzy giggled.

Lo loved her laugh. Through all the cheating, he had a soft spot in his heart for her. Every time he spoke to her or when they were together, she would put butterflies in his stomach.

"I'm in Puerto Rico, at my grandmother's house. We landed yesterday. I tried to call Kim a few times to see if you was around, but you wasn't. I'm glad that you're there now. I missed you so much."

"Sorry, Jazzy. I've been in and out of here, but I missed you too. When you coming back, and why didn't you just call my phone?"

Jazzy got quiet before she spoke in a soft sorrowful voice. "My grandmom wants me to stay for the summer, and when I did call your phone, it went straight to voicemail."

Lo's stomach turned. "The whole summer? Jazzy, I miss you. Do you know that I walk by your mother's house all the time hoping that you stick your head out the window, or walk out the door to go to the store or something?" He could hear through the phone that Jazzy was breaking down. They were young, but they really had feelings for each other.

"I'm sorry, Lo. I hope that I don't lose you."

"Don't worry, Jazzy, I'm not going anywhere." Lo could hear her grandmother in the background calling her.

"Lo, I have to go. We are going to the beach. I'll send you some pictures of us there. I love you, Lo."

At that moment Lo really felt like he was in love with her. Even though he was still messing around with Jenny, his feelings were strong for Jazzy. "I love you too, bye."

"Bye, Lo!" The lines went dead.

The whole afternoon Lo's mind was clogged up with Jazzy. The only thing that distracted him was when he went to pick up more work from Rock. After chopping, he walked past Jazzy's house, hoping that she popped her head out the window. He got to the corner of East Turner and Carlisle and saw Jenny sitting on her porch. He decided to walk over and see what she was doing. He walked up to her and gave her a kiss on the cheek. She was surprised by his antics.

"Damn, your girl leaves and all I get is a kiss on the cheek."

Lo was caught off guard with that comment. "I'm sorry. I wasn't sure if you wanted to kiss me or not, but since you insist," he replied, leaning over again, this time kissing her on her soft, beautiful lips.

All the bitterness and feelings he was feeling about Jazzy went straight out the window. Jenny had the softest lips he had ever felt in his young life, and there hadn't been many. After that, they chilled for a couple of hours, kissing and talking about random stuff. Not once did he even think about Jazzy.

Lo headed back to the park to hustle. He had fourteen hundred dollars' worth of crack in his pocket. He bought a half ounce off of Rock for $500, and he kept $30 in his stash. In Lo's mind he knew that this would be the start of his takeover. In the next half hour, he sold twenty dubs and made $380. Not including the fronts. Lo knew he wasn't supposed to front a fiend, but he felt like they were the ones bringing in the money. He was determined to make all the money he could, so he took all that came his way. His plan was to take over and control the block. For three days, Lo was out all hours of the day. He was trapping hard, nonstop. Money was coming in fast. He was down to his last fifteen dubs. In the first two days he had enough money to re-up but was indecisive as to what to do. He couldn't ask Mack what to do, and all Rock told him about was half ounces and ounces. Lo had no clue what came after that. So to save money, he bought another half ounce off Rock. He was still young and new to the game.

~ ~ ~

"Breaking news: There is new information on the homicide that took place in the south side of Allentown.

The victim was a seventeen-year-old young man from Easton. Thomas Smith was shot twice in the chest while sitting in the passenger seat of an SUV, driving through the Cumberland Gardens projects. Witnesses say they heard multiple shots then another weapon going off. Police are investigating the possibility of more than one shooter. At this time there are no suspects. Anyone with information, please contact the Allentown Police Department. This is Sharon Stone reporting live from Cumberland Gardens.

"Thomas Smith from Easton?" Mack mumbled to himself as he clicked off the news. "Who the hell was that? Could that be one of Zeus's people that he tried to rob?"

To Mack, it wasn't making any sense. He grabbed his gun and headed to the barbershop. Mack had a chip on his shoulder. Since his sixteenth birthday, he had almost been killed twice. He thought that it was a birthday gift from God that he was still alive. He decided to test the waters. Instead of going to see his personal barber, he decided to walk into Rico's shop. All eyes were on him as he walked through the door. He felt the tension, but he paid it no mind. He walked up to the first barber that was cutting some dude's hair.

"How many people do you got, bro?"

"One more after him, then you're next," the barber told him. Mack sat down in the waiting area for his turn to come up. A couple of minutes later Rico came out of his office to check out the new customer. He locked eyes with Mack and walked back into his office. Mack could see the double-sided glass that sat behind Rico's saltwater fish tank. He knew that Rico was watching. After a half-hour wait the barber pointed his chair in Mack's direction. He stood up, walked over to his chair, and sat down.

"Two on top, blowout," Mack said.

The barber began cutting his hair immediately. While cutting Mack's hair, the barber got a call on his cell phone. Mack was watching him through the mirrors. The barber's facial expression caught his eye. He seemed confused as he tried to pass Mack the phone.

"It's for you," the barber said, still wearing a confused look on his face.

"Who the fuck is that?"

"It's my boss. He would like to talk to you."

"Tell him to bring his ass out of the office and stop hiding behind that two-way glass."

Mack immediately pulled out his Desert Eagle and

placed it on his lap. He was born for this type of drama and never ran from it. He knew there was tension and wanted to face it head-on. Rico stepped out of his office and nodded to Mack, telling him to come into the office. He told the barber that his cut was on the house. Mack had no idea what was going on. He started questioning himself, wondering if Rico knew he ran with Ricky. Or did he know that he robbed one of his workers? Mack didn't care; he was ready to kill something.

When his cut was finished, he walked over and entered Rico's office. He felt sorry if somebody was waiting behind the door, 'cause he was going to light up something terribly.

"I'm Rico," he said as he stuck out his hand to Mack.

"I know who you are," Mack replied, shaking his hand with a firm grip, keeping the other one on his waist where his gun sat.

"Calm down, Mack. I just want to talk business with you."

"So what's up?"

"Look, Mack, I've been hearing a lot about you. Your name came across my path."

"And how is that?" Mack asked, interrupting him.

"Let's just say that you deal with a close friend of mine. He told me you're a loyal spender. A kilo here and there. How about we make some real money together?"

Only one person came to mind when Rico spilled the beans. DIESEL! "Oh yeah, what else?"

"Don't you wanna know who gave me that information?"

"Nah. I just want to know why I am in your office," Mack cut straight to the point.

"I heard that you are an animal and you like to put in work." Rico went into his desk and pulled out a brown envelope. He opened it up and pulled out a picture. Mack thought that it was Ricky. "We both got twenty grand for this guy's soul."

Mack took a glance at the photo sitting on the desk. He knew exactly who it was. "And when do you need this done by?"

"Take your time, but the sooner the better. Depending how I feel at the time, I might give you interest."

Mack didn't care about no interest. This hit was personal. If Rico would have come to Mack's without money, he would have done it for free. But a payday only put a smile on his face. Mack took down Rico's number and said that he would call him when it was done.

Mack stepped out of the barbershop looking fresh to death. He knew that this could be his chance to link up with a real boss. A favor for a favor in Mack's eyes. He headed toward his Jeep with a plan already on his mind.

~ ~ ~

"AR, here's a G-pack. Bring me back seven hundred."

"Damn, Lo. You out here making moves and shit."

"I'm just trying to stay above water. Let's go to George's. You think he will sell you some dutches?"

"I don't see why not. Olga always serves me."

AR bought three dutches and a soda; then the duo went to C-Lo's spot to cop a twenty sack. C-Lo always hooked the young boys up when they bought weed. He went in his bag and grabbed a handful of bud and gave it to AR. They sat in the park and sparked up.

An hour later the whole park was jumping. Logan came out with his basketball, and the old heads came out to sell their drugs. Some came with their own L's and passed them around to everyone. Money was coming in by the hundreds. At that time, everyone knew that Lo was selling dubs. No one cared though. It was all part of growing up in the Hole. Eventually you became a product of your environment, and hustling was the product.

All day he posted up hustling. On the days it rained, he stood posted up under the money tree. The tree sat on Bradford Street, which kept the hustlers dry. It was a beautiful night, and the park was lit up from all the lights on each end of the park, and the lights from the project buildings.

In the summer when the streetlights came on, most of the hustlers would post up on the steps and roll dice all day. The night one of the old heads, LG, came to gamble. He had invited one of his old heads, his dad's friend, to the hood to shoot dice. LG was a gambling fanatic. He enjoyed the dice games, but his twist was craps. It didn't matter which game he played; he had no flaws.

LG pulled out three stacks to gamble. Each point was for twenty dollars or better. Lo and all the goons watched the game. He believed LG took some losses, but most of the time he came out on top. He was a live wire. He did time in SCI-Huntingdon when he was eighteen for selling drugs, but never learned his lesson. The minute he came home he was back to trapping. His father was a big-time hustler who had gotten indicted by the Feds in the early

'80s, when the crack epidemic hit the streets. From afar, Lo could tell that LG was uncomfortable, or he was losing. He pulled out his 9 mm and placed it on the steps. The old man panicked.

"Nephew, put that piece away," the old head said as he shot the dice, hitting his point.

That was five straight points. LG was down five hundred. Then he looked at Lo.

"Young boy, hold this down while I take this old head's money."

Lo jumped off the stoop, grabbed the nine, and placed it on his hip. LG pulled out a cigarette, lit it, and took a puff. Lo could tell that he was flaming. Lo felt invincible. He had a big-ass gun on his waist, a pocket full of dubs, and crunched up dirty money.

After LG smoked the cigarette, the momentum changed in his favor. It was like some kind of voodoo spell or something. He raised the stakes to $100 an ante. Within six rolls, LG was now in the old head's pockets. Ten minutes later the old head was down five hundred, then a stack. Altogether, LG took twenty-seven hundred dollars off his old head. He started yelling.

"Who wanna fuck with the God LG? Who, huh?" LG

said, holding the wad of cash up in the air for all to see.

LG looked over to Lo and signaled him to bring him his strap. Lo hopped off the stoop and passed his old head the gun. LG then walked his old head to his car as they chatted about the next game.

"Young fella, you only took back what you lost last week."

LG laughed. "I know, but I had to make a show on my home turf."

He gave his old head a hug and closed his car door. Twenty minutes later, LG returned to the park with two cases of beer. The whole hood was out drinking and celebrating life, just enjoying the days on earth. That was the norm in the Hole. Getting high, getting drunk, rolling dice, playing ball, fucking bitches, and getting money.

# FOUR

**IT'D BEEN A COUPLE OF WEEKS SINCE THE LAST TIME MACK** had seen Princess. She started college, and he was busy in the street life. He was feeding everybody. Big Poppa was buying a couple of ounces off him. He also snatched up a couple of guys from the Hole. He had the Gardens on smash.

Things had been going good with Diesel. He kept his word and was consistent with the work. But Mack knew if he could somehow cut off the middleman and go directly through Rico, his income would triple. He knew the game, and he couldn't get too greedy. That's when people start to hate. Jealously and envy would start to fill in people's minds. Mack was cool. He would just wait for his opportunity.

He was already moving a brick a week. A kilo wasn't a lot, but for some reason it took Diesel a little longer for Mack's order. Mack figured that he was getting his work fronted and had to pay off his debts before he could fulfill his order. So he analyzed things and plotted his target.

Mack received a little information from Rico and some

information from Diesel. Nowadays you have to be careful who you say certain things to because you never know who's plotting on you. He was way ahead of his time. He knew the art of war and played his enemies closer than flies on shit.

Mack pulled up to the house on Main Street in Northampton with Junito in the passenger seat. He explained the plot to him weeks in advance. Junito was like a pit bull who hadn't eaten in days, starving for blood. He was hungry to let his slugs fly into his victims. When his slugs tasted blood, he got aroused like a vampire feeding. He wore his devilish look. His eyes were bloodshot red, and he didn't even smoke today. That was the true definition of the devil inside. It was thirty minutes past two in the morning when Mack got the call.

"Mack, are you still hungry, because food is on its way."

"Starving," Mack replied.

"Food is going to be served with a sexy female. Twenty minutes, enjoy." The call went dead.

Mack looked over to Junito. "Twenty minutes, he's with a female."

Junito stood mute. Mack checked his chamber making sure that he had one in the head. Ever since he touched his first gun, he kept one in the chamber. It was an old habit to check every time. Junito kept his snub nose tight in his hand on his lap. He looked at Mack.

"Put it away. I'll handle this on my own."

Mack refused to let Junito handle his business, but he insisted. Mack then explained to him that he needed this man dead. FLATLINED. Not only was this a personal hit, but it was also a business hit. Junito knew that if shit hit the fan, he would eat the case for Mack so he could continue his business.

Out of nowhere, a dark blue Suburban pulled up to the Main Street house. Junito hopped out of the tinted-up sedan and walked toward the parked SUV. It was dark on Main Street. There were no streetlights on and no one in sight. The white neighbors had a curfew. They'd be in their third dream by one o'clock Mack did his homework.

Junito grabbed his .357 inside his Nike hoodie. His hands were sweaty, but his nerves were calm. Junito noticed the man hop out of the driver's side and was trying to be a pure gentleman as he attempted to open the passenger door. A loud blast echoed through the quiet neighborhood.

BOOM!

Junito let off the first shot into the man's back. His back arched as he hit the truck. The Haitian lady screamed as she saw the masked gunman approaching. Junito's eyes locked dead into the female's face, and he raised his index finger over his lips gesturing for her to keep quiet. He placed the barrel of his .357 to the head of his target and gave him Rico's message.

"This is for Johnny. NEVER BITE THE HAND THAT FEEDS YOU!" Then he let off a shot to his head.

BOOM!

The female screamed as blood and brain matter splattered on her face.

BOOM! BOOM! BOOM!

"Good night, bitch," Junito said, hitting her three times in the chest.

He quickly ran back to the car where Mack was waiting for him. Soon as he had half of his body in, Mack hit the gas, peeling off into the night.

# FIVE

LO WAS FEELING HIMSELF TO THE MAX. IT WAS THE FIRST day of high school and was fresh to death. He had on a pair of fresh white Air Force Ones, Enyce pants, with the T-shirt to match. He had a chain around his neck that was iced out, swinging back and forth as he walked. While walking from class to class, he bagged two Puerto Rican girls from the south side. When he exited the school, he noticed his squad at the steps next to the field. As he approached his team, he noticed a few of them had tears in their eyes.

"Muzzle, what's going on?" Lo asked, concerned.

"Somebody killed Zeus outside of his house last night."

The first thing that came to his mind was Mello. "What's up with Mello? Where he at?"

"Mello is good. He's at his crib with his mom and sister."

Lo's mind was all over the place. He had a great day at school, and then he came out and got hit with this bad news. One of his old heads just got bodied. He needed to get up with Mello and make sure that didn't have anything to do with him.

Muzzle started shedding more tears as he explained to Lo that Zeus was killed along with his girlfriend. He said that Zeus's girl was hit three times in the chest, and Zeus once in the head. He was so emotional that he couldn't control his anger.

"Somebody gotta die."

The entire school had their eyes on the niggas from the Hole as the crowd got bigger. They could tell that the hood just lost a soldier. After each member and female from the Hole got together, they headed back to the projects. Everyone was in shock about the news. No one could believe it. But just like Mack always told Lo, there's no love in this game. It's either death or prison, and Zeus was a casualty of death.

Lo walked to Mello's house, knocked on the door, and waited for him to come out. Before Lo could say anything, Mello hugged him tight and started crying.

"They killed my father."

Lo was hurt with Mello's words. This was the first time he had to deal with the death of one of his homies, and it had happened to his friend's dad. He knew that there was nothing he could say to ease his heart.

"Just be strong, Mello. We all are here for you. Anything

you need, we got you. We gonna find out who did this. Come on, let's take a walk."

Lo and Mello headed to the park, where they met a crowd of loving friends. People from across town came out to give their condolences. When Mello got near, everyone greeted him with hugs. Family and friends filled the park to support him. Lo could see it in his eyes that he wanted to kill the person that was responsible for killing his father, but he was just a kid trapped in a man's world.

As the day dragged on, there were a lot of stories going around about how Zeus was killed. But no one had any facts to support it, just a bunch of assumptions.

~ ~ ~

**In The Gardens**

Ricky was in tears as he explained the situation to Mack.

"Calm down, Ricky. You're overthinking shit."

"Mack, I'm telling you; he knows. We gotta kill him first."

"How do you figure that Rico killed Zeus?"

"That day he ran up on us at the hotel. He told Zeus that he knows he sent someone to rob his runner."

"Ricky, don't you think if Rico knew Zeus robbed him, he would have killed him then? Why wait a month later?"

Mack had a point, Ricky thought, but he still felt like Rico was involved. Mack knew that he had to calm Ricky down. If not, it was possible that he would try to kill Rico. From afar, Mack saw Junito walking down the street. Every couple of steps, he would look back to make sure no one was behind him. He walked up and gave Ricky and Mack some dap, then whispered in Mack's ear.

"What the fuck is all the secrets about?" Ricky was already feeling some type of way.

Junito, sick of Ricky's shit, landed a solid hook to his jaw. Ricky stumbled back a few steps as he ate the unexpected punch. Ricky followed with a flurry of punches. Junito dodged the first two, but the third and fourth connected. Then the two started wailing punches. Blow for blow, they each connected.

Mack watched his closest goons knuckle up and laughed. He had known that this day would come. It was long overdue. He loved them both, so he let them fight. After a couple of minutes, Mack went into his waistband and pulled out his gun. He didn't like wasting bullets, but he knew this was a time he had to. He pointed the gun in the air.

BOOM! BOOM!

The two killers stopped instantly as the shots echoed through the hood.

"You two done now?" Mack yelled. "Y'all like two bitches. That's enough of the bullshit. Y'all got your shit off your chest, right? You better had. We ride together, not separately. We're a team. We don't need no animosity in our team. That's how empires crumble, and we're not gonna crumble. Y'all good?"

Both men nodded their heads and shook hands, and then Ricky said, "Now let's get the fuck out of here before the cops come."

On the way to Jessica's house, Mack's phone rang. He moved away from Ricky and Junito and answered the call.

"Hello." After he heard the voice of the caller, he couldn't help but smile.

"Good job, Mack. Come to the barbershop in twenty minutes, we have some business to talk about."

Before Mack had the chance to say bye to his goons, they were already in Jessica's house. He hopped in his Jeep and headed over to Rico's shop. He dreamed of this day. He knew that he had an opportunity to deal with the boss and connect directly. He didn't want to jump the gun. His business with Rico was to kill Zeus. He didn't say anything about supplying him yet, but Mack would make sure to bring it up.

As Mack pulled up to the front of Rico's barbershop, he noticed the crowd of mourners outside of Big Poppa's spot. They were still mourning the death of Zeus. Mack decided to keep his car moving and circled the block. He parked on the side of the barbershop. Rico was already waiting for him at the side exit door. Mack exited his car, jogged to Rico's shop, and entered the office.

"First, I would like to know how you found out where Zeus lived. I've sent out my best men to find that nigga's location, and he managed to slip through the cracks every time."

"I have a very good team and we keep our ears to the streets," he replied, not revealing anything.

"I see, I see. I wouldn't want to be on your bad side. Anyways, I'ma man of my word, and you got the job done."

Mack watched as Rico carefully picked up a briefcase and placed it on top of his desk. He started fiddling with the combination. After a few moments, the briefcase opened. You could smell fresh, clean money inside. Rico then spun the briefcase around toward Mack.

"Here's $20,000 in cash and a kilo for your services. But there's one thing," Rico said.

"One thing?" Mack replied, gripping his waist.

"Calm down, Mack. As of today, we are bonded for life. Now I'ma be your supplier. You don't have to pay for work. You're on my team now. Anything you need, it's yours."

Mack acted like he was surprised with the news, but he knew by finishing the job he was given, that he would be in Rico's circle.

"So what can you get me?" Mack asked. He knew it was a stupid question, but he wanted to see where Rico's head was at.

Rico laughed. "Well, Mack," he said while shaking his head, "I know you move about one brick, maybe two a week, and your supplier Diesel, he problems supplying you. So to start, I can give you five joints on the arm at eighteen apiece. That's ninety thousand. You think you can handle that?"

"That's a small thing to a giant. What else can you get

me?" Mack laughed.

"What else do you need?"

"In my hood we got a strong demand for some good weed, but it has to be the best around. I like to have the best."

"No problem, Mack. Let me make a few calls, and I'll get back to you in a couple of hours. In the meantime, take this briefcase. Every made man needs one. Then finish what work you have and let me know when you're ready for the five. The combination is 7-21-14."

Mack shut the briefcase and gave Rico a businessman handshake. "I'll be waiting on your call."

He left the barbershop with a smile on his face. He knew from here on out, he would be sitting on top of the world. No more dealing with the middleman. On top of all that, he didn't have to come out of his own pocket. It was all on the arm.

He was about to have all this work. He needed a new spot. He thought about venturing to another town. If he did that, eventually people would talk. Mack was confused. He didn't want to slip up like all the other drug dealers that came before him and landed in prison.

"I gotta think long and hard," he said out loud. "Naw, I just gotta get out of town."

# SIX

ZEUS'S FUNERAL WAS PACKED TO CAPACITY. ABOUT THREE hundred people attended the fallen soldier's going home party. His family wanted everybody to dress casually, but his family from the Hole didn't know what casual meant.

In the days leading up to the funeral, everyone in the Hole placed orders for RIP T-shirts. So each member from the Hole had a Rest in Peace shirt with Zeus's picture advertised on the front. On the back they had an airbrushed saying, "Only the good die young. Rest in peace, OG Zeus."

After the funeral was over, his immediate family had a dinner in respect for him. The Hole had their own party and celebration. There were cases upon cases of beer stacked up in the park. They also had mad weed circulating throughout the place. In the hood all across the world, this is how gangstas paid their respect. The park was filled with mourners sharing funny stories about Zeus.

Police knew all about the homicide, and the mourners didn't try to hide it. The fence that surrounded the park was filled with Rest in Peace Zeus shirts, so the police didn't come by harassing the mourning project. Even though a funeral was still going on, drugs continued to be sold, and money was still being made.

Lo stood close to Mello. He treated him like a little brother. Mello was only twelve, but his mind was as sharp as a mature eighteen-year-old's. He knew what would be expected of him to help his mom survive through the difficult times ahead. And that was to get into the game and hustle like everyone else was doing to feed their family. He was going to continue his brother's legacy.

Since the death of Zeus, Lo and Mello had been chatting about making money. Mello needed someone to front him some work, and Lo was the one that he ended up turning to for some help.

"Lo, you think you can put me on?" Mello came right out and said. He had a serious face.

"You know I would. As soon as I re-up off of Rock, I got you."

"Damn, Lo, I need something now. My mom gotta pay rent."

Lo was almost out of work. Before Zeus's death, he had bought an ounce and only had twenty dubs left. He was wondering what happened to all the money that Zeus was making before his demise, but he didn't want to ask right now.

"How much is her rent?"

"Three hundred dollars."

Lo went into his pocket and pulled out three hundred dollars and placed it in Mello's hand. "Here, give this to Mom Dukes."

Mello didn't say anything. He just gave Lo a hug. "Thanks, bro."

"It's nothing," Lo said as he went into his other pocket. He pulled out a sandwich bag that contained his twenty dubs. "Here's twenty dubs. Get on your feet, bro."

"You sure? Don't you gotta re-up?"

"Yeah, but it's cool. Rock wants to front me some work anyway. I'ma be straight, and when he does, I'ma hit you off again."

Mello couldn't believe his eyes. Lo gave him his last dubs and three hundred dollars. He knew that Lo was a loyal friend. Ever since that day, he considered Lo to be his brother.

# SEVEN

MACK TOOK TIME OFF OF HIS BUSINESS AND COLLECTED ALL the money he had in the streets. He was sitting on $186,000. He felt like he was on top of the world, but he knew there was a lot more money to be made.

He had to determine how much and what he wanted to pay his top employees. He wanted to make sure that his team was happy and everyone ate. Therefore, he split the cuts evenly, regardless of how much work each person put in. Mack cut everyone twenty grand. Juice, Vic, Husky, Rob, and Ricky. Since Husky and Vic had to split the proceeds, he planned to give them extra on the re-up. Mack was left with $160,000. He placed the six grand inside his pockets and put the hundred in the briefcase that Rico gave him.

~ ~ ~

It'd been almost two months since the last time Mack saw Princess. Even though they spoke to each other daily, it wasn't the same as touching her. Since he was taking some time off, he decided to pay her a surprise visit. Before heading to New York, he booked a hotel suite in the Poconos for the two. Then he hopped on a Greyhound bus to New York. Within a couple of long hours, he arrived at Princess's doorstep.

Mack was anxious to knock. It had been so long since he felt the love from his beautiful girlfriend. Before knocking, Mack had a plan and dialed Princess's number.

"Hi, daddy," she answered cheerfully.

"Hey, baby, what are you doing?"

"Nothing, just got out of the shower and getting ready to go eat breakfast."

"Did you get the gift I sent you through UPS?"

"No, I haven't gotten anything. When did you send it?"

"I sent it yesterday morning. Overnight delivery." The minute he told her about the package, he rang her doorbell.

"Wait, Mack, the doorbell just rang. That might be my gift now." Through his phone, Mack could hear her running to the door, breathing heavily. "You still there?" Princess asked.

"Yeah, I'm still here."

"Hold on, let me open the door." The minute Princess

pulled the door open, she couldn't believe her eyes. Tears started flowing down her face as she dropped her phone and jumped into Mack's arms. She squeezed him so tight that he nearly lost his breath. "Why didn't you tell me you were coming?"

"It was a surprise," Mack said as he picked her up off her feet and carried her back into the condo.

He took her straight to her bedroom, undressing her, and giving her what she hadn't had in a while. Her body was still flawless. He pushed her legs open and started eating her pussy.

"Mmmmmm! Oh shit! That's right, eat it, baby," she moaned as he licked and sucked on her clit.

He then got up and sat next to her on the bed. He pulled her up on to his lap, positioning her pussy in line with his rock-hard dick. Before inserting it in her wet hole, he started jerking it up and down with his right hand so Princess could see its full length. Her pussy quickly got even wetter at the sight of it. He stroked it a few more times before inserting it deep inside her love tunnel.

"Yeesssss, daddy," she moaned as she bounced up and down on his shaft.

They went at for about an hour before they both came

in unison. Mack lay back on the bed as Princess lay on his chest.

"How did you get here?"

"Greyhound!"

"Why didn't you tell me to pick you up?"

"I knew you were too busy, and I wanted to surprise you. I got something special for you."

"You do. What is it?" Princess said excitedly, cutting Mack off.

"Plus, I wanted to get out of town."

"Is everything okay?"

"Yes, ma, everything is fine. Enough of me, are you ready for your next surprise?"

Princess nodded her head in excitement. She was so happy to be with Mack right now that she really didn't care about any other surprises. As she was driving, she thought that she could get used to Mack being with her in New York. She knew that most likely wasn't going to happen though. He had a business in PA. Every day she was reminded of just how much he reminded her of her father. She was just praying that he would get out before it all came crumbling down.

"Mack, where are we going?"

"We gotta go to the Poconos. I gotta see someone at the Pocono Palace Resorts. It's near the outlets."

"I know where it is. My father has a timeshare there, but at the Royal Resorts."

Princess's eyes glowed as she opened her hotel room door. The tall champagne glass jacuzzi stood right in her face. She felt like a queen as she looked at her king.

"This is all for you, my beautiful queen."

Princess grabbed Mack by the hand and pulled him into the hotel room.

~ ~ ~

Mack had a wonderful weekend with Princess. Everything was flawless. When she dropped him off at home, she left with tears in her eyes because she didn't want it to end. She wanted him to come back to New York with her, but he had refused. Mack had just started making moves with Rico and had to manage his operation. In the drug game, the more money people make, the more they tend to slack off. They're not hungry anymore. Most of them wanted thousands, but Mack wanted millions.

Mack stopped at Rico's barbershop unexpectedly. When he entered, Rico was in one of the barber's chairs, getting a cut. He sat in one of the empty chairs and told him about his time away. Before Mack could finish his story, shots rang out from outside. POP! POP! POP! POP! POP! POP! POP!

Bullets ripped through the barbershop's glass. One bullet hit Rico's barber in the shoulder. He dropped his clippers and hit the floor. The bullet just missed Rico's head. Mack jumped out of his seat and covered Rico's body with his, acting like a human shield. Rico's bodyguard ran out of the barbershop, gun in hand, but it was already too late. However, he did notice the sedan speeding off down the street.

"Rico, esta bien?" asked the bodyguard as he walked back in.

"Si."

"Mack," Rico called out, trying to remove the dead weight off his body.

"Rico, I'm hit," Mack said, forcing the words out of his mouth and gasping for air.

Rico quickly rolled Mack off of him. Blood was all over the barber cape. Mack didn't move as he breathed intensely. As he lay there, Rico grabbed some towels and put them on Mack's stomach, trying to stop his wounds from bleeding.

"Mack, stay with me," Rico said, seeing him go in and out of consciousness.

Within minutes police and an ambulance EMT arrived. The barbershop was riddled with bullets. The EMT placed an oxygen mask on Mack's face as they tended to him and strapped him on a stretcher, then rushed him out to the hospital. They called into the emergency room.

"We are on our way with a teenage male, multiple gunshot wounds to the back and stomach area. ETA, approximately five minutes," the EMT bellowed over the radio.

~ ~ ~

"Hello," Maria said as she answered her phone. "Yes, this is her . . . WHAT?" she yelled through the phone and then hung up. "Lo, get down here."

Lo walked down the steps wondering what was going on. He knew it wasn't good. "Mom, what happened?" he asked.

"Your brother's been shot."

Lo's heart nearly stopped as tears came out of his eyes. Maria rushed to the hospital, running every light until she reached the emergency room.

"Can I help you?" asked the receptionist.

"Yes, my son just came in. His name is Mack Ortiz. He was shot. I need to know where he is and some information on his status."

"Can you fill out these forms, please?"

"Fuck those forms. Can you tell me what's wrong with my son?"

"I'm sorry, ma'am, but your son is in surgery. He is in critical condition. I have no other information at this time. Now can you please fill out these papers so we can better help your son?"

Maria could hear a commotion coming from the rear of the hospital as a couple of doctors rushed to the operating room. "We're losing him; we're losing him," one of them yelled.

Lo knew that they were talking about Mack. Tears poured out his blue eyes. Mack was doing bad, and he couldn't do anything about it. Neither of them was religious, but he started praying. As Lo was finishing his prayer, the hospital doors swung open. He turned toward the door just in time to see Husky rushing in. Behind him were Juice, Ricky, and Junito. Word must have spread throughout the hood.

When they saw Lo's watery eyes. That's when they realized that it must be bad. They all shook their heads with tears of their own coming down their cheeks. A few minutes later, Rob, Jessica, and Princess came busting through the door.

"What happened?" Princess said loudly. "I just dropped him off."

Maria looked at Princess as she was crying, wondering who she was. She had no idea that Princess was Mack's girlfriend.

"Ms. Maria, this is Princess," Jessica said with tears in her eyes. "She's Mack's girlfriend."

"Hi, Princess," she said. "Sorry we're meeting like this. They're not giving me any info. The only thing they said was that he's in critical condition."

She didn't tell them about the commotion she heard just minutes earlier. Juice and Junito were flipping out while Husky and Ricky stood in shock. Husky just paced back and forth anxious to find out who shot Mack.

"Why was Mack inside Rico's shop?" Ricky said out loud.

Ricky had no idea that Rico was Mack's new connect. The only ones that knew were Juice and Junito. They both kept quiet. Juice thought, for Ricky to be so close to Mack, he didn't seem to worry about him. He was only worried about why Mack was in the shop. Juice knew that Ricky wanted revenge for the death of Zeus, so he kept his eyes and ears on Ricky. An hour later a doctor exited the back of the hospital into the emergency room.

"Can I speak to Maria Ortiz?"

Maria jumped to her feet. "Yes, I'm Maria, Mack's mother."

"Can you please come with me."

Mack's family knew that wasn't good news. Loud sobs came from everyone. Maria dropped to her knees.

"No, tell me what happened to my son right now."

The doctor helped Maria back to her feet. "It's okay, Maria. Your son, he's a fighter. He's a strong young man who has the will to live. He's stabilized now. We almost lost him, but he's doing good now. He had been shot twice, once in the stomach and once in the back. The bullet from his back hit his lung. Luckily the thick glass from the business slowed the impact down from the bullets."

"What type of bullet?" Junito asked, interrupting the doctor.

"From the look of the fragments, it came from a high-caliber handgun. My guess, a .45, .50 cal. Detectives have to do the ballistics."

Ricky got defensive quick. "How certain are you?"

"Like I said, son, it's in the detective's hands now. But for now, only two at a time can see him. You have to be very quiet in the ICU room. He needs some rest. He's lost a lot of blood."

Maria looked in Princess's direction where she had been crying since she arrived at the hospital. "Princess, come on, honey. You should come in with me first."

~ ~ ~

Three days went by, and Princess was right by Mack's side, only leaving to use the bathroom or shower and change clothes at Jessica's house. She took care of him every minute. She fed him three times a day, and at night she snuck him McDonald's and Wendy's. Mack had trouble breathing due to his asthma and damaged lung, but she was there to encourage him.

Maria showed up each day after work to check on her son, and each day she arrived, Princess was sitting there by his side. Maria barely had a chance to speak to her alone, but this day was perfect. After a long day at work, Mack was asleep, and Maria invited Princess to the hospital's cafeteria for something to eat. Since both of them were hungry and Princess knew she wanted to know more about her, she accepted the offer. Once they were seated, Maria wasted no time getting straight to the point.

"So how long have you been seeing my son?"

"I met him at his birthday party at Jessica's house. I've known Jessica for years. We used to live next to each other in New York. She's my best friend."

"Oh, you're from New York?"

"Yes, the Bronx."

"What do you do?"

"Right now, I'm in college. I go to the University of New York. I'm studying to become a pediatrician. In four years, I'll have my bachelor's, and eventually I plan on opening my own pediatric clinic."

Maria smiled. "I see my son found him a special lady."

"Thank you!"

"Do you see a future with my son, you know, with all the stuff that's going on with him?"

"To tell you the truth—" Princess paused for a moment to collect her thoughts "—I've been trying to get him to come stay with me in New York, but he's so stubborn that he won't listen to me. I guess he loves Pennsylvania too much to just up and leave."

"I think he gets his stubbornness from me," Maria chuckled.

"I know the lifestyle Mack's living in. It only leads to death or prison. Let's be real, Maria. This is the second time that Mack has almost been killed. I love your son, and don't want to see anything happen to him. I'm afraid that one day I will get a call like the other day, or even worse, someone telling me that Mack is dead or in prison." Tears filled up Princess's eyes.

"I see you really do love and care for my son. I understand and wish that he would take your advice before it's too late. Knowing my stubborn son, he won't stop. Ever since his father went to prison, sorry, stepfather, he demanded to be the man of the house."

Maria paused as her own eyes got watery. Princess passed her a napkin. "He doesn't realize that everything he's doing, his baby brother Lo is trying to follow his footsteps. I was cleaning Lo's room the other day and found fifteen hundred dollars under his bed."

"Oh my God," Princess said, already knowing where this was heading.

"I know Mack isn't giving him any drugs to sell, and I haven't given him that kind of money. I'm afraid I'ma lose my kids to these streets," Maria began to cry harder.

Princess scooted over to the chair next to Maria and comforted her. They were beginning to form a bond as if they were family.

"It's going to be okay. I will keep talking to Mack until he comes around," Princess told her.

The conversation ended with tears in both of the ladies' eyes. They finished their dinner, then went back to check on Mack.

~ ~ ~

A week went by, and Mack was finally released from the hospital. Princess was right there by his side the whole time. He asked her to stop at Rico's barbershop. She seemed confused but didn't question her man. She had heard Ricky wondering why Mack was at Rico's. She even thought to herself the same thing.

Mack had revealed to her that he and Ricky robbed Rico's worker, but she knew from her mother to never ask questions when it came to business. As Princess pulled up, Mack noticed Rico had his front window replaced. The shop looked like it had never been touched. Rico had hired more security that stood outside the barbershop, looking like the secret service.

Mack hopped out of his girl's Lexus and slowly walked to the shop's entrance. He was approached by Rico's new bodyguards. They realized who Mack was as he lifted his head up from the ground, revealing his face. As soon as he entered the shop, the entire place got silent. The barber that got shot pointed to the office as he looked at Mack. The days that Mack had been hospitalized, Rico sent his goons to check on him and make sure he and his family were okay. Once Mack entered the office, Rico stood up and gave him a soft hug.

"Thanks, Mack, for saving my life."

Mack smiled in pain. "It's only right. I'll die for mines."

Rico smiled at the gesture. "How's the wounds healing?"

Mack didn't speak. He just took off his shirt and showed Rico the scars.

"I'm okay. Just in a little bit of pain. Did you get any word on the shooter?"

Rico sat down in disappointment. "Nothing solid." He then went into his desk drawer and took out Mack's Desert Eagle. "Look familiar?"

"Fucking right." Mack smiled as he grabbed his gun and put it on his hip.

"I couldn't let you go down with that."

"Good looking for taking that off of me and putting it up. So where were we? How's business?"

"Good. I held them five for you. My peoples got back to me about the marijuana. I got one hundred pounds for you."

"What's the numbers on that?"

"Three hundred each."

"Good. That sounds like music to my ears," Mack said.

He knew that he was about to make major moves. Before his weekend getaway with Princess, he had Juice contact a few of his peoples he grew up with in Bethlehem. Mack needed to extend his reach. Allentown wasn't big enough. He needed to expand to open up the flood gates even more.

"Give me an hour, and I'll have someone drop it off," Rico said.

"Say no more. I'll be waiting."

~ ~ ~

After Rico's drivers dropped off the work to Mack, he took Princess to Jessica's, where he was planning to meet up with Juice and Junito. They were surprised to see Mack fully recovered, but they hugged him gently while giving him dap.

"Anything new about the shooting?" Mack asked.

"No, but your boy Ricky been acting funny. The night of the shooting, he was only concerned as to why you were at Rico's barbershop and what type of bullet hit you," Juice stated.

"I think he shot you," Junito chimed in.

"You think? Well let's not jump to conclusions right now. Juice, you talked to your peoples in Bethlehem?"

"Yeah. They're in the process of getting rid of what they

have."

"Aight bet. Did you finish the work?"

"We have a hundred grams left of it. That should be gone by tomorrow."

"Good. I just got right and got hit off with a hundred pounds. So let's holla at Fat Freddy and tell him we need to talk business." This was Mack's time to take over. With his prices, no one could compete with them. "Tomorrow at noon, I'll be ready. Tell everybody to be around to get their packs. Juice, I got a different game plan in my mind. Instead of me doing the packs, I'ma just give you the whole joint at a set number and you do you."

"Say no more, cuz. Whatever you want to do."

CHAPTER 8

Early Saturday morning while Maria was at work, Lo was awakened by the sound of banging glass. He got up to check on the unfamiliar noise. He peeked in Mack's room and stood frozen at the sight he saw. It was Princess asleep looking as beautiful as a queen could look. Lo slowly closed the door, not trying to wake her up. He headed down the steps toward the kitchen. When he entered, he saw Mack over the stove with a hospital mask on covering his nose and mouth.

"Mack, what are you doing?"

He was caught off guard, surprised at Lo's presence. "What's up, little bro? Just cooking up this raw."

Lo didn't get what he was saying, but the smell upset his stomach. He ran back upstairs, checked on his stash, and then jumped in the shower.

He finished his shower in a half hour. He hopped out of the bathroom and noticed Mack's bedroom door was open. Lo poked his head in and saw Mack fumbling inside a duffle bag. Mack looked back as he felt a presence watching him.

"What's up, bro? Get dressed; we need to talk," Mack said.

"Aight," Lo replied. He went back to his room and got dressed quickly, not knowing what Mack wanted to talk to him about.

He threw on some pants, a wifebeater, a Polo shirt, and some sneakers. He slapped on some deodorant and a dab of cologne. Lo was only smelling good for Princess. As soon as he entered Mack's room, he was complimented by her. His face turned red.

Mack laughed then got serious as his face switched up.

"Mom told Princess she found $1,500 under your bed. Before you say anything, be honest and tell me what you been doing."

Lo was caught off guard. He was a bit shocked, but he knew this was coming, and he had to keep it real with his big brother. Eventually Mack was going to find out anyway.

"I've been pushing crillz in the Hole. I found a couple of twenties in the park."

"What?" Mack said, cutting him off.

"I moved them and kept getting a re-up. Now I'm at fifteen hundred. I think I did a good job. What you think?" Lo said, trying to crack Mack's cold stare. He knew Mack wasn't going to agree with him hustling. He knew that he would be upset about the whole thing. Lo could tell that he was disappointed, but what did he expect? It was only a matter of time before he would get into the drug game too.

"You know this isn't the life that I wanted you to be caught up in."

"I, I, I know but . . ."

"But nothing," Mack said, raising his voice. "Do you

know the consequences to this game? You'll end up dead or in prison. No one makes it out. No one. Only one in a million, bro. Your chances are slim. Who's supplying you?"

Lo knew if he told on Rock that would start a war. It didn't matter though because Mack was going to find out, so he kept it a hundred.

"I get my work off of Rock."

"Rock, Diesel's cousin?"

"Yeah. He fronts me ounces."

Mack was surprised that his little brother was moving ounces. He thought that he was pushing grams or balls.

Lo continued speaking. "Mack you probably think that I don't know what I'm doing, but I studied all your moves while I was in the Gardens. Why do you think I was up there all those times? I was only up there to scope the scene and how you ran things. I took what I saw, and now I have a team of goons working for me. I barely do hand-to-hands. I got AR and Mello moving everything for me. In a few years with the right connect, I'ma have the whole hood buying off of me. The same way you do."

Now Mack was the one caught off guard. Lo sounded

just like he did. He looked at Princess and just shook his head. He knew he showed his little brother too much. Princess didn't get involved. She knew this was a brother-to-brother talk. She just sat there listening with a surprised look on her face also. "This kid got some brains. I just wish you would have put it to use in those books, but who am I to judge? I'm not innocent myself. I showed you the way. Since you had Rock supplying you, giving him all your hard-earned money, I gotta deal for you. First, what do you give AR and Mello?"

Lo smiled. He smelled the money about to come in. "I give AR packs. He pays me $700 off each pack. So out of an ounce I will make between two stacks and twenty-four hundred. Then I gotta pay Rock eleven hundred. Mello, I just put him on."

Mack knew that Rock was head cracking his little brother, but that's all part of the hustle. Mack went into his duffle bag and pulled out a black bag.

"Are you ready to make real money, lil bro?"

Not in a million years would Lo have thought that Mack would put him on. He figured if he didn't get it off of Mack, most likely he'd get it off of Rock. "Yeah, I'm ready."

Mack pulled out his scale from under his bed and placed

it on his dresser. He placed his hand in the bag and pulled out a big chunk of crack, then sat it on the scale. He went back in the bag a couple more times. He grabbed a sandwich bag and placed the work inside.

"Here's two ounces. Bring me back $1,200. If anyone wants weight, tell them you can get it at $29 a gram, and I'll give you part of the cash. I also have weed, so if you see C-Lo, tell him you can get pounds for him for $700. If he gets ten or more it'll be cheaper."

All this time Lo knew that Mack was making moves, but he didn't know that he was holding weight on everything. He was a connect on the rise, and Lo was his underboss. By time he turned sixteen, he was hoping to be in his brother's position.

~ ~ ~

It was exactly noon when Mack pulled up to the Gardens. He parked in Jessica's parking lot. When he hopped out, he noticed Lori standing at her front door, looking beautiful. "Where's Ricky?" Mack asked as soon as he stepped into Jessica's house where the rest of his team was waiting.

"We haven't seen him since that night at the hospital," Juice said.

"Since the hospital?" Mack was surprised. He thought that was strange because Ricky hadn't checked in on him either. "Aight, I'll look for him. Until then, Juice handle Ricky's corner. I'ma change things around here. No more packs. I'm going to give you a whole joint. Break it down evenly between the fellas. Bring me back $28,000. When you get a hold of your aunt's man in VA, tell him that we can give it to him at twenty-five and the weed at six a pound."

Juice broke everyone off evenly, 250 grams a piece. On a breakdown they could easily bag up 1,200 dubs. That's over twenty grand if sold without taking any shorts. Mack left Jessica's and stopped at Isabel's before heading to Big Poppa's spot. No one answered at Isabel's, so he left a note for Ricky:

Ricky, I stopped by to check on you. I

texted you but you didn't reply.

Get a hold of me as soon as possible.

Mack

Mack pulled up to Big Poppa's house. He could tell by his face he was still mourning Zeus's death. Mack knew he didn't have a supplier, so he offered his help.

"How much can you handle?" Mack asked him.

"I should be able to move a brick in a week. But I told you I'm tapped out."

"I know you're hurting, but how does thirty sound for the brick on the arm?"

Big Poppa started rubbing his hands together. "I can handle that. I'll make some calls."

~ ~ ~

An hour later Mack pulled back up with Princess. He exited the car with a small duffle bag. As he entered the house, he noticed that Big Poppa was counting money.

"What's up, big boy? I see your back."

"Nah, just getting by. Here's $8,000 toward the thirty. I have people waiting." Mack liked what he was seeing from Big Poppa. He went into the duffle bag and pulled out a brick and placed it on the table.

"I brought you something extra. Here's ten pounds, $750 each. That's $7,500 for the ten. Altogether 29.5."

Big Poppa was shocked again. "Mack, I couldn't thank you enough. Let's make that an even thirty for the lookout."

"Say no more." Mack gave him some dap before walking out the door.

He knew his reach in the drug game was expanding. A few more heavy hitters and the city would be his, he thought to himself as he hopped back in the car with Princess.

# NINE

ALTOGETHER LO CHOPPED UP 275 DUBS. IF HE SOLD IT himself, he could make $5,500, but he was spreading the love with his team. He would be making the least, so he kept 25 dubs for himself. He headed to the Hole on foot. He stopped at AR's house first. As he entered his room, AR was blasting Rick Ross out the house speakers. Lo threw the bag on his lap. AR smiled as he continued singing. He finally lowered the music and asked what was in the bag.

"Twenty-five hundred dollars worth. Bring me back seventeen fifty."

AR didn't say a word. He hopped off his bed and started to put on some clothes. He was anxious to hit the block. Lo told him that he had to go to Mello's, and he'd see him in the park. As Lo walked up to his screen door, he noticed Mello's mom posting up Zeus's obituary on her kitchen window. Lo could tell that she was still taking his death hard. He could hear Zeus's two dogs running around the basement as he knocked on the screen door. The door swung open, and Mello stood there with a small smirk on his face.

"What's up?"

"Put some sneakers on and come outside. I got something for you," Lo said.

Mello quickly slid on his shoes and came outside to holla at Lo.

"How's everything going, Mello? How are you holding up, bro?"

"I'm okay, but I really miss my dad, man."

"I know how you feel. I haven't seen my dad in a long time. I haven't even gotten a letter from him since he's been in prison. Besides that, how you do with the dubs?"

"I moved them the same night you gave them to me. I made $140."

Lo was happy to put some money in his friend's pockets. He dug in his pocket and pulled out a pack. He placed it in Mello's hand. Mello quickly put the pack in his pocket to make sure that no one saw the transaction. "What's in there?" Mello asked.

"There's $2,500 worth. Give me $1,750."

Mello was excited. He went back into his house to stash the work.

"What did you bring out?" Lo asked.

"Ten dubs for now."

"I got twenty-five on me. Let's go to Kate's so I can stash some."

After Lo stashed the work, they hit the park. Instantly a fiend came and wanted $150 worth. Mello and Lo split the sale. Four dubs a piece. They each made $75. An hour went by, and between the two of them, they each made a total of $760. Lo was left with seven dubs, so he let Mello make the rest of the sales that came through.

By the end of the night Mello almost moved a stack. AR was nowhere to be found. Lo spotted him earlier walking down E. Linden Street toward George's. He figured he was stuck on Cutthroat Island. The old heads hated when young boys posted up there. They saw all the fiends before they could make it to the park.

It was almost 7:30, and tomorrow was a school day. Lo and Mello walked to the store before it closed. As they approached, AR was posted up with his dope fiend cousin Ace. Ace got hooked on heroin when he was sixteen. He never was able to recover from it.

"What's good, AR? Where have you been? Mello and I had the whole park to ourselves. No one was out, and we made over a stack today."

AR went inside his pocket and pulled out a knot of money. "Here's $750. I owe you a stack."

"Damn, you made all this on Cutthroat Island?" Lo asked as he counted the money.

AR laughed. "Not all of it, but most of it. Ace got me a $200 sale from his cross-town fiend."

Lo placed the money in his back pocket. He didn't want to mix it up with the $380 that was his and the $600 Mello gave him. Lo walked into George's, bought a bag of chips, a turkey and cheese sandwich, and an iced tea for his walk home.

# TEN

"WE NEED TO TALK," A FEMALE'S VOICE SAID THROUGH THE phone.

"What is there to talk about?"

"I haven't gotten my period in three months. I think I'm pregnant."

Mack's heart stopped for the first time in his life. He could not believe the words he was hearing. Mack was warned not to mess with her, but he couldn't resist the temptation. He was speechless right now. All he could think about was Princess and how he was going to explain this to her.

"Are you sure it's mine?"

"Are you serious, Mack?" Lori shot back. "Do you think I'ma hoe? You're the only one I've been with."

"Come on, Lori. We only had sex once."

"That's all it takes, Mack. You no good piece of—"

Before she could finish, Mack interrupted her. "Relax, relax. I didn't mean it like that. Look, set up an appointment with the doctors, and we'll find out if we're pregnant."

"Okay, Mack."

Before Lori could say another word, Mack hung up the phone.

"I can't believe this bitch Lori talking about she's pregnant," Mack said out loud to no one. Then he brushed the thought aside. He already had his mind made up. If Lori was really pregnant, whether it was his or not, he would talk her into getting an abortion.

Two days later, Mack and Lori pulled up to Lehigh Valley Hospital for her checkup.

"Hello, Lori Martinez. How are you feeling today?" the doctor asked.

"I'm feeling fine."

"Any morning sickness at all?"

"No, not so far."

"Have you taken a pregnancy test?"

Mack was getting frustrated with all the questions. He wanted the pregnancy results right then and there, but the doctor was just trying to drag shit out.

"No, I haven't. That's what we are here for."

"Okay then. First things first. We need to get a pregnancy test done and do an ultrasound to see what we can find. Are you okay with that?" asked the doctor.

"Yes," Lori replied.

Lori took the pregnancy test and gave it to the doctor's assistant. The doctor came in the room to do her ultrasound. With further evaluation, the doctor then got out of her chair and gave Lori a dry napkin to wipe the gel off her stomach, then exited the room. Lori and Mack were confused, as the doctor didn't say a word before she left. Mack had his thoughts, and inside he was smiling. A few minutes later, the doctor returned.

"I'm sorry, Ms. Martinez, all the test results came back negative. It shows no signs that you were ever pregnant. It is uncertain as to why you haven't had your menstrual cycle in three months. We scheduled an appointment for you so we can see why."

Tears sprung out of Lori's eyes. Mack felt bad. Even though he was jumping for joy inside, he placed his arm around her, comforting her. She was speechless. She signed the doctor's papers and they left. As Mack drove toward the south side, he was hungry and took Lori out to eat. Mack parked at Red Lobster, and Lori was shocked.

"Is this a date?" she asked.

"Yes, a friendly date."

Lori thought Mack was a pure gentleman, but he didn't want to leave her on bad terms.

"I'm sorry I wasn't pregnant," Lori said.

"It's okay. I didn't think we were ready to have a kid anyway."

"I know, Mack. I was afraid to tell anyone. It's been three months; eventually my belly would have shown. So, I felt I had to tell you first."

"I'm glad you did. You know I would have been there for you and the baby," Mack lied. He didn't want to tell her that he was planning an abortion.

"It's okay, Mack. I know you would have. We don't have to worry about that anymore. So why haven't you hit me up? You just wanted some pussy?"

"Nah. It's not like that. I just been so busy. I got a lot going on right now."

"Yeah, I heard that. I also heard that you got shot. Are you in some kind of trouble?" Lori asked, trying to be sincere.

"I'm okay. It was an accident. It wasn't intended for me. I was in the wrong place at the wrong time." Mack quickly changed the subject. "So how's school?"

"Well, I start my college classes next month. I'ma major in nursing and business."

"That's what's up. You can be my own personal nurse."

"If you want me to," Lori giggled.

Mack and Lori had a good dinner. He used his fake ID to order two Coronas, and two shots of Henny for himself. Since Lori wasn't pregnant, she ordered two Long Island ice teas. They sat in the restaurant talking about their summer. They had lost track of time and drinks after the first two. By seven o'clock, they were feeling nice. As Mack pulled up to the back of Lori's crib, his head was spinning from mixing beer with liquor.

"No one's home," Lori said as if she was trying to invite Mack in her house for some homemade dessert. "I think my mom is still at church. They won't be back until nine. Too bad you have to handle some other business."

Lori was throwing shots at Mack, and the liquor in his system was kicking in big time. In one ear the devil was talking to Mack, saying he better tear that pussy up again. And in the other ear, an angel was telling him not to do it, because his girl would kill him. He was confused. By that time, Lori already made her move. She placed her hand on Mack's dick and started whispering sexy Spanish words in his ear.

"Ay, papi. Tu quiero esto *(You want this)*?"

Mack was getting turned on by her sexy exotic voice. His dick was hard as a rock. Lori continued to seduce Mack by nibbling on his ear. He had enough. He grabbed the box of condoms out of the glove compartment and let Lori lead him inside her crib.

He sat on the sofa as Lori straddled his lap. She knew just what he would like. She started slowly kissing him as she took off his shirt, while Mack gripped her ass. She grinded slowly on his dick. He unsnapped her bra and started licking on her nipples. They were hard and pointy. She let out a soft moan as he licked and sucked on them. Her pussy was wetter than a faucet. He unbuttoned her pants, and she stood up and pulled them down.

She had on a black lace thong. She turned around so he could get a clear view of her ass. She slowly bent over and slid down her thong like a stripper. Mack quickly slid off his pants and boxers. As he attempted to put on a condom, Lori stopped him.

"There's no way I'm going in this girl raw again," Mack thought to himself. Lori was thinking about something else though. She got down on her knees and took his dick into her mouth.

Mack's eye's widened as she gagged on his dick. His toes curled up as he felt himself about to explode. Lori laughed as he pulled her lips off his manhood.

"Is that too much for you, papi?"

Mack didn't respond. He wanted to fuck the shit out of her now because her head game was vicious. He got up and slipped on the condom and bent Lori over on the sofa. He slowly slid inside her tight, heated walls. He could tell that she hadn't been fucking anyone else because her pussy gripped to his dick like a suction cup.

The liquor must have kicked in full throttle because Mack was fucking Lori like a dog in heat. She screamed out loudly as he went deeper and deeper inside her walls. She was taking everything he threw at her. Her legs quivered each time she had an orgasm. They were so into it that they failed to hear the back door open.

# ELEVEN

*October (One Month Later)*

EVERYTHING WAS GOING GOOD IN THE HOLE. MELLO, AR, and Lo were doing numbers. Between the three of them, they were clearing two ounces in a good week. There was one time when they moved over two ounces in two days. The old heads were mad because the young boys stood on Cutthroat Island taking all their business, but they respected their grind. The young boys knew if they chilled in the park to hustle with the old heads, they wouldn't be able to make money because the fiends would go straight to them. So a few hours a day, they chilled on Cutthroat Island.

After making a couple of dollars, Lo and AR decided to enjoy the money and take a trip to Dorney Park. It was close to Halloween, so the park was filled with Halloween decorations for the festival. JP decided to tag along with them and took Kim. Lo and AR wanted to take Jenny and Jessica, but Jenny was out of town with her mom, and Jessica wasn't feeling AR.

So instead, AR took Carmen and Lo took Sandy. Lo

knew that he was wrong for taking her, but he had no one else to take. Mello and Logan came along without a date. They planned on bagging a couple of chicks at the park. They all jumped on the bus on Hanover Avenue to Whitehall Township.

Dorney Park was like two big amusement parks connected to each other. One side was the regular park with all the roller coasters and other rides. Then on the other side was the water park and other water rides. It was called Wild Water Kingdom. Lo loved the roller coaster. As a child he never had a chance to go there, so he made it clear that when he had enough money, he would enjoy the park himself.

They had a new ride there called Steel Force that was just built last year. The line damn near went out of the park. Before they got in line, they stopped at the Lazor. At one time that was the best ride they had there.

Sandy was terrified of roller coasters, but they all forced her to get on and to just close her eyes. Once locked in the car, her eyes began to tear up. The Lazor went into motion, and she quickly grabbed hold of Lo's arm. As it started climbing up the tall mountain-like rail, Lo was anticipating the sixty-foot drop and felt Sandy's nerves as she held his arm. He told her to relax as he placed his arm around her shoulder.

As they reached the top of another drop, Lo released his arm from her shoulder and grabbed her hand. As the cart was about to go over the drop, he squeezed her hand and launched it in the air with his. Sandy screamed out her lungs as they hit the drop at full speed and twirled through the first loop.

Then came the second one. The cameras flashed. Lo laughed through the entire ride as he held her arm in the air. Sandy was shaking and in tears. Once they got off the ride, Lo gave her a comforting hug. He wanted to show her that he cared. Sandy took advantage of the moment and gave him a wet, juicy kiss. Lo was caught up in the moment and kissed her back. He felt his crew staring and whispering behind him. They didn't pay them any mind as their tongues intertwined. After the kiss they walked to the picture booth holding hands.

Lo and Sandy's picture was the funniest. He had both of his hands in the air screaming, while Sandy had one arm forced in the air, while the other one was trying to cover her face. Lo bought the picture for Sandy and made a keychain out of it.

After the ride, everyone split up in couples while Mello

and Logan went girl hunting. They all planned on meeting up at the horse carousel at the entrance when the park closed. Lo and Sandy went around playing games. They spent forty-five minutes at the ring toss game trying to win a giant Tweety Bird that she fell in love with. He spent nearly fifty dollars more than the actual stuffed animal cost, before he won the prize. Win or lose, Sandy didn't mind.

All she ever wanted at that moment was to spend time with Lo. Everything else was a plus in her book. She grabbed the stuffed animal and said, "I'ma call you Lo." He just laughed at her joke, but she was serious.

After that they went to war with each other. They jumped on the horse race. The key to the game was you had to shoot water through a toy gun into a target. As you hit the target, the horse moved. Once the bell rung, Lo shot directly at the target. His horse shot out to the lead. He knew he would win, so halfway down the race, he started to aim poorly so Sandy's horse could catch up. Her horse ended up winning the race.

Sandy raised her hand in victory. She won a Bugs Bunny stuffed animal. Once they left there, they grabbed some ice cream and sat on a bench that was located near the bumper car ride. The couple got into a deep conversation.

"Lo," Sandy said, looking into his eyes. "Why don't you pay any attention to me?"

"What do you mean?"

"I mean, I'm sure you know that I am in love with you, but you never want to give me the time of day."

"What do you mean? We went out before."

"I know, but that was in elementary school. Now that we are older, I want to be in a real relationship with you. I really love you."

Lo had ignored the first I love you, but Sandy said it again, and this time she put feelings into the words. He didn't think she felt like this. He thought she was infatuated with him, not in love. "But I'm with your cousin Jazzy."

"So, what was that kiss about?" Sandy asked, getting in her feelings. She had a point, but he loved Jazzy and wasn't about to lose her over something as stupid as a kiss.

"I wasn't going to turn down a special kiss from you," he replied with a sensual smile.

He got that from his father. He had a great comeback

that left Sandy blushing, but she had a comeback of her own. She leaned forward and kissed him again.

"So did you enjoy that one too?" Sandy asked, flirting with him.

"Did I?" Lo said sarcastically. "You're lucky people are around, or I would tongue you down right now."

It seemed like Sandy knew what he was going to say because the second the last word fell out of his mouth, her come back came quick.

"Well there's no one around now."

Lo couldn't back down on his words. So he went in for the kill, not worrying about Jazzy or anyone who saw them. As they sat on the bench, they locked their tongues together for five minutes. When they were done their lips were swollen from all the sucking they had done. Lo believed he had made Sandy's life sparkle.

"The night isn't done," Sandy thought to herself. She had a special surprise for him that only she knew about.

They all met at the entrance when the park was closing. Sandy held her two stuffed animals while Lo held the basketball and football that he won at Hot Shot and QB Zone. Danny and Tete happened to be at the park. He offered them all a ride home in his mom's minivan. During the ride, they decided to end the night at the Red Roof Inn and throw a little hotel party.

After dropping off Logan, Mello, AR, and Carmen, Danny picked up Muzzle, Terry, Tay Tay, and Danny's girl Crystal. Since Danny was over eighteen, he rented the rooms. One was for JP and Kim, Muzzle and Tay Tay, Terry and TeTe, Lo and Sandy, and one for himself.

They all chilled in Danny's room drinking and smoking, having a good time. After the weed and liquor were gone, they all went their separate ways. Lo took a quick shower trying to bring down his high. As he got out, Sandy jumped in. Lo felt like he was about to have sex with Sandy.

He was anxious, but he didn't expect anything because she was a virgin. When she came out of the shower, she walked into the room with only a towel on covering her body. She quickly jumped under the covers. Lo could feel her nerves as he touched and kissed her.

"Wow," he mumbled as he felt how soft her body was.

Her body was trembling. After a while, her nerves were calm. She touched his erection then placed the condom on. The rest of the night was magical for the both of them. Afterward, they slept like babies.

# TWELVE

**HUSKY AND VIC WERE MAKING POWER MOVES ACROSS** town. During a visit at Vic's sister Janet's house, they noticed a lot of fiends running around Second Street. As they posted up at Janet's house they stuck their noses in. The first night they set up shop, together they made $500. They hit a gold mine, they thought to themselves. For the last couple of weeks, they were cutting throat. During that time, a few of those Second Street niggas caught wind from a few of the fiends that some niggas had posted up across the street inside an apartment on Cumberland Street and were making sales. Sick of the shit, they approached Husky and Vic from across the street.

"What you niggas doing on our block?" one of the Second Street niggas shouted.

Vic, not knowing the rules, responded, "This ain't your block. This is our block."

They immediately got into a verbal argument, shouting from one side of the street to the other. Vic got under their skin, and they walked away ice grilling the Cumberland soldiers. Vic was from New York, so things were different.

In New York there wasn't any talking. Niggas got killed for pumping on another man's block. He thought that those Second Street dudes were sweet, so they continued pushing work on their block, not knowing that they were about to start a lifetime war.

It was a nice sunny day, mid-November. The temperature was a little warmer than usual. Husky was visiting Janet when a group of Second Street goons jumped out on him.

"You one of them niggas from the south side coming down here trying to take our money?" asked Mark.

Even though Husky was surrounded by six gang members, he did not back down. He looked around and noticed that Janet was watching it all. He saw that she was already on the phone calling for backup.

"Yeah, I'm that nigga. So what you saying?" Before Mark could speak another word, Husky stole him. Mark dropped unexpectedly. He didn't even see the punch coming. Husky turned, pivoted his foot, and punched another nigga before the other four goons were on him. He tried to fight all six of them until Janet came running off her porch with a bat, swinging wildly. They all dodged the bat, running away.

Husky stood up laughing because he had no marks or bruises from the fight. Mark was gushing out blood from his nose, talking shit to Husky. As the police cruiser drove by, the Second Street niggas scattered. Moments later, Mack pulled up with Juice and hopped out of the car ready for action. Husky explained the situation to Mack and Juice. For three hours they stood posted up waiting for any of them to show back up.

The night was still young, so after they all showered, they met up again and decided to go to the after hour. Mack, Husky, and Juice knew that they were going into Second Street territory, but they didn't care.

"They were just trying to bag a couple shorties."

The moment that they pulled up to the scene, Husky spotted Mark and the other dudes that jumped him. He pointed them out as they drove by. Mack and Juice strapped up before hopping out the rental they copped from a fiend.

They felt the tension as they walked toward the crowd. Mark noticed Husky and started waving his hands, screaming at him. Husky, with no fear, called Mark out in front of everybody. Mack and Juice posted up right next to Husky, one on each side. Instead of fighting, Mark, showing off, pulled out a small gun. All they could see was a little bit of the chrome in Mark's hand. Then he began waving it side to side. The southside niggas just laughed at the entertainment.

"In the streets, real niggas don't pull out unless they are going to use it. Stunts like that will get you and whoever else killed."

"These niggas ain't no threat." They turned around and headed toward their car to avoid any problems or witnesses.

The minute they turned their backs to Mark, he raised his arm and let off a warning shot in the air.

POP!

Instantly, Mack and Juice pulled out their guns, spun around, and sent shots into the crowd.

POP! POP! POP!

BOOM! BOOM! BOOM!

Everyone started scrambling for cover. Mark hit the ground after the first shot went off. He lay flat on the pavement while everyone scattered. They thought he was dead. They ran to the car and left the scene in pandemonium.

"Fucking cloud killer," Mack said, driving away from the scene.

~ ~ ~

"Breaking news: An eighteen-year-old Allentown man was transported to Lehigh Valley Hospital Cedar Crest late last night with three gunshot wounds to his chest. The teenager is listed in critical condition, fighting for his life. Reports say multiple gunshots were fired around 11:45 p.m. outside of Fat Cats nightclub. The witnesses say an argument erupted when a man pulled out a gun and fired in the air. Witnesses say that two assailants then returned fire. Police are looking for two suspects. They are known to be brothers, sixteen-year-old Mack and nineteen-year-old Husky Ortiz. Anyone with information on their whereabouts is to please contact Allentown Police detectives immediately. They are considered armed and dangerous. This is Susan Morales of CBS news signing off."

Lo's world came crashing down as he watched the news for a second time. The police were looking for his brothers for an attempted murder, possibly murder charge. He thought that he would never see them again. His mind started spinning as he sat on the sofa crying.

As Lo got to the Hole, everyone was talking about

Husky and Mack. They knew Mack was a gun. It was just a matter of time before he got himself caught up in a situation. Lo could tell from everyone's expression that they were happy that Mack was a wanted man. They were scared of him.

Jealousy and envy showed on all of their faces. Lo left the park because he felt the hate around him. He headed over Mello's house to vent.

"Lo, what are you going to do if Mack goes to prison?" Mello asked.

"I don't know." A million and one things were going through his mind, and it scared him.

At school everyone was chit-chatting about Lo's brothers. It gave him a good reputation. His brothers were wanted on attempted murder charges, and his classmates respected that. Lo walked through the hallways with his head held high, not showing his true feelings. His brothers were still on the run, and he didn't have a clue what his next move would be.

~ ~ ~

The past week Mack had been hiding at Vic's sister Pebbles's house. She lived a half a block away from Second Street on Linden. Still business was run in the

Gardens, while Mack made all his runs during the evenings.

Princess heard about the shooting from Jessica. She rushed down to be with her man. Husky hid in the Hole while Vic held down their corner. When Princess arrived at Pebbles's house, she was upset. She kept it ladylike. She knew the game, and this was part of it. Some people get shot, some die, and some go to prison. Mack apologized to her for getting himself caught in a mess.

"You don't have to apologize, Mack. You gotta stop getting into shit though. You just got shot, and now this. The Feds are probably all over you right now."

Mack kept his head down as Princess was blunt with him. He knew that she was right. She learned a lot about the game from her father.

"I think I'ma have to go on the run."

Princess interrupted him. "On the run? Are you crazy? I am not going to be watching my back, looking over my shoulders. You have nothing to worry about, Mack. I talked to my dad's lawyer. We have a meeting with him on Monday morning."

BOOM!

A loud bang came from the front door. "Police, everybody down."

Mack was caught slipping. He knew that his time on the run was over. He looked into Princess's watery eyes and whispered, "I'm sorry."

"Police! I said get down." A couple of SWAT team officers jumped on Mack immediately.

"We got him," another officer yelled through his radio.

Princess bawled as they arrested Mack. She had never been in a raid before.

"Don't say nothing, babe. I'ma call the lawyer," she said as she watched them escort Mack out of the house.

~ ~ ~

"Where's the gun at?" the good detective asked.

"Just tell us who the shooter is," the one known as the bad cop said.

Just by their questions, Mack knew they didn't have anything on Husky or Juice. He was in the interrogation room for two hours getting beat up with question after question.

"You think you're slick?" the bad detective yelled. "We

know you're the one supplying weight around the city."

Mack just yawned. He knew his rights. He knew that at any time he could ask for his lawyer, but he wanted them to work. The lead detective got mad at Mack's emotionless attitude. He punched Mack in the face.

"Are you done yet?" Mack finally spoke. "I'm trying to bail out. Charge me already."

They took Mack to booking. He was charged and arraigned on one count of attempted murder and other related offenses. The judge set bail at $50,000. Mack called Princess and told her how much his bail was with the 10 percent. A half hour later he posted bail.

"Hey, baby, did you miss me?" Mack smiled as he walked out of the county prison. Princess grabbed him and gave him a hug.

"The lawyer said to give him a call soon as you get out. Here," she said, passing him the phone.

"Hello, Attorney Rossi and Firm," the receptionist said.

Antoni Rossi was one of the best defense attorneys in New York. His firm beat 95 percent of their cases. Rossi and Firm were a judge's worst nightmare. The New York state prosecutors wanted no smoke with them, and soon the Lehigh County prosecutors would get a taste of what they could do.

"Can I speak to Attorney Rossi?" Mack asked.

"Hold on one minute."

"Hey, Mack, it's Tony. Welcome home. I heard all about the incident. Have they scheduled a preliminary date for you yet?"

"Yeah, it's December 7 at 9:00 a.m."

"Okay, I'll be down there. Make sure you keep your nose clean and stay out of trouble."

"Say no more. So how much are we talking?"

Rossi laughed through the phone and asked Mack to return the phone to Princess. Rossi said a few words to Princess, and then she hung up.

"How much is he going to charge me?" Mack asked.

Princess shook her head. "Nothing, pa. He's been paid for years by my father." She walked to her car, unlocked the doors, and sat inside, waiting for Mack to join her. "Mack, you're coming to New York with me. I can't continue to get these calls. I'm afraid that the next call I'ma get is you getting killed."

Mack wasn't in the right mind to argue. He had too much on his mind. So, without thinking, he agreed to go.

# THIRTEEN

MACK'S BUSINESS WAS FLOWING. RICO STEPPED UP THE work from five to ten kilos. He had points on each side of the city, and Juice started pushing work in Bethlehem. Mack headed to Jessica's to tell everyone that he would be going away for a while. He felt like he was bringing too much heat to his team and didn't want to jeopardize anything.

Mack knew that the detectives were onto him from the questions they were asking. He also knew that his team wasn't involved with the cops. He didn't know where Ricky was most of the time. He sensed a change in him since he had got shot. So when Mack finally did run into him in the Gardens, he pulled him aside.

"Damn, bro, where have you been?" Ricky asked.

"Where have I been? Nigga, where have you been? We were in a war, and you were nowhere to be found. That's not like you."

"Sorry, bro. I heard about that, but I've been home taking care of Mom."

"You sure? I left a note at the crib for you to hit me up,

and I still haven't heard from you. You didn't even answer my calls or text messages."

"I never got it, and my phone has been fucked up for a minute," Ricky replied.

"Aight. Well I'm heading out of town for a while. Contact Juice if anything comes up."

Ricky got in his feelings quick. "Contact Juice? For what? Who Juice? I've been here from the beginning, from the robbery, until now. Now I'm being treated like a flunky. Fuck that."

Mack felt disrespected at the way Ricky was talking to him, but he let it slide and walked away. Everyone heard Ricky snapping at Mack. Juice was ready to pop off, but Mack gave him the look to fall back. Ricky walked away in the opposite direction from where Mack's crew was.

Mack told everyone that he'd be back, he needed to clear his head. He drove straight to Isabel's house to see what Ricky was really up to. She gave him a hug and kiss.

"How are you doing, Izzy?"

"I'm okay, but Ricky's not here."

"I know. He's in the Gardens. I wanted to ask you what's been going on. Ricky said he's been taking care of you.

Something happen?"

"Taking care of me? What? Ricky didn't tell you?"

Mack looked at Isabel confused. "Tell me what?"

"Ricky got arrested six weeks ago. He served vice 150 grams. His bail was $100,000. He said that you bailed him out."

"Two weeks ago." Mack was concerned about Ricky. Why didn't he mention it to anyone? He wondered if that was how the detectives knew about his drug dealings, but he was arrested for an attempt, not drugs. "Okay, Izzy, don't tell Ricky that I stopped by. I'll see him in the hood." Mack left.

"I hope Ricky ain't snitching," Mack said out loud. "I gotta warn Juice."

Mack called Juice, but he didn't answer. Mack left him a voicemail. Since he was on that side of town, he stopped at Rico's barbershop.

"Look who the devil brought in," Rico said as Mack entered his office. "What's going on, Mack? I thought you was smarter than that."

"I know, Rico. The dude jumped my brother then tried to stunt at the club. He shot first in the air, so I retaliated and returned fire."

"Do you have a lawyer?"

"Yeah, he from the city. Antonio Rossi."

Rico's eyes lit up at the name of Rossi. "How do you know about Rossi?"

"Should I be concerned?" Mack asked with a concerned look on his face.

"No. He's a mob lawyer. One of the best in the business. How did you get a meeting with him?"

Mack was confused but on point. Rossi must be a beast if Rico couldn't even get close to him. "Let's just say a friend of a friend."

"Say no more. If I need him, plug me in. I'm sure you will spank the case. Especially with Rossi. You have to be extra careful bringing that high-profile lawyer into this town. Police are going to look at you like you're big time."

"I know. That's why I stopped by to tell you that I'ma stay low until my case is over. But I need you to supply me for at least three months."

"Where are you going?"

"I'm thinking about going to Florida. Enjoy some sun,"

Mack lied. There were rules to this game. Never let anyone know your next move. He wanted to lay low.

"How much are you going to need?"

"Like twenty-five bricks and two hundred pounds. I will have the money that I owe you on Sunday before I leave. Will you be ready by then?"

Rico laughed. "I'm ready now. By the way, I got word on the person that was shooting. He's now working for vice." The first person that came to Mack's mind was Ricky, but he let Rico continue. "My bodyguard seen a blue Toyota peeling off the day you got shot. We did a little research on the Toyota."

When Rico mentioned the blue Toyota, it hit Mack like a ton of bricks. Isabel had a blue Toyota. Ricky used his mom's car to put in some work. Was he out of his fucking mind putting her life in jeopardy like that?

Rico continued, "We found a blue Toyota that is owned by her." He pulled out a picture of Isabel.

Mack's heart was beating so fast that he thought he was having a slight heart attack. That's when he knew that Ricky had put his mother's life in danger. He knew something was up with Ricky, but never would he have thought that his man would become a snitch, and snitch on him, at that.

"And she has a son name Ricardo. He goes by Ricky."
He immediately showed Mack a picture of Ricky. He was definitely on top of his game when it came to finding out things. "Also, Ricky and that piece of shit Zeus robbed one of my workers for money and drugs. Ricky was around here bragging about it. One of my barbers' customers informed him about it. That bitch also had the balls to come into my fucking business and rob me and put this scar on my head. The neighbor saw him leaving out the back of my shop, pulling off his ski mask and running down the street. I got eyes all around this block. Do you know Ricky?"

Mack was caught up in an awkward situation. He wasn't sure if Rico knew that Ricky was his right-hand man. If he said no that he didn't know Ricky, and Rico knew, that might discredit his loyalty in Rico's eyes. Now if he said yes, he knew Rico could have him killed. Mack played it cool and gave himself a little more time to think.

"You said that he was an informant?"

Rico was thrown off for a second, but he fell for the bait. "Yeah. He served vice 150 grams and he gave up valuable information."

"Are you sure he only gave up valuable information?"

"Hold on!" Rico jumped on his cell phone and dialed some numbers. He then placed the phone on speaker. A lady appeared on the line.

"Narcotics Division. Can I help you?"

"Mari, it's Enrique. Fax me a photo of your new informant. All his paperwork and statements."

"No problem, papi. Give me a minute."

After a couple of minutes, the fax machine came alive. Mack couldn't believe his eyes. It said Ricky's real name, PWID 150 grams to Det. Lake. Arrested September 17. Released November 10 on unsecured bail. Then a photo of Ricky. The third fax paper came through. Mack saw it with his own eyes and Ricky's signature and the names he said that were involved in drug distribution. Rico, Ninth Street barbershop. Rock, Diesel, Big T from the Hole, Big Poppa, Pretty Boy.

The list of names just kept going. Juice, Vic, Rob, Gardens. Mack's blood was boiling. He wanted to kill Ricky. He had to. If not, then everybody was going to prison. Mack jumped on his phone and dialed up Juice. Still there was no answer.

"Mack, do you know Ricky?"

He couldn't lie. "Yeah, I know him. We grew up together. He knows everything about me, except who my connect is. He don't know that I do business with you."

"We have a mole that needs to be dealt with."

"Don't worry, Rico. I'ma kill him."

Rico tried to speak, but Mack stormed out of the barbershop. He called Princess. "Be ready," was all he said, then hung up. He was furious. Not only did Ricky try to kill him, but he also tried to set everyone up. Then Mack thought about Isabel. He hopped on his phone and called Rico, but no answer. Two seconds later, Rico called back.

"Mack, are you okay?"

"Yes, I'm good. The mom, Isabel. Leave her alone. She's like a mother to me."

"Are you sure?"

"Yeah, positive," Mack ended the call.

Mack texted Diesel and informed him about Ricky. He had no time to spare. Before he picked up Princess, he drove by the Hole. He hopped out of the car and jogged to the park. He was greeted by thirty people.

"Did you see Rock or Diesel?" No one said a thing. He stopped at Diesel's mom's crib, but he wasn't there either, so he left a message. "Call me as soon as you get this. No one serve Ricky."

Mack jumped back in his Jeep and headed to the Gardens. He spotted Vic and Husky as soon as he pulled up. "Jump in," he told them. "Did you see Juice?"

"Yeah. After you left, him and Ricky went to handle something."

# FOURTEEN

IN THREE MONTHS DEALING WITH MACK, LO MADE CLOSE TO nine stacks. If he didn't have runners, he probably would have made even more. He rolled up a dutch, and before he lit up, he bagged up his last ounce. He added two more people to his team, Fena and Miguel. Fena was a pure hustler. He was built for the game. He was a wild Dominican but was born and raised in Puerto Rico.

He just came off the island and barely spoke good English. Fena was smooth with his mouth and had a natural hustler's gift. He could sell salt to a slug, water to an ocean. So no matter what Lo gave him, he moved it.

Now Miguel was the total opposite. He was quiet and barely spoke to anyone in public. Some say that he was traumatized as a child when he witnessed his cousin getting gunned down. The good thing was no one would ever expect him to be a hustler.

Lo was in his thoughts trying to figure out who would be getting what, when he heard his name being called.

"Lo!"

"Who that?" he said, getting up off his bed and walking

into the hallway.

"It's Mack. Come to my room."

"What's up, bro?" Lo said, greeting him with a hug and dap. "What the hell happened? Are you going to prison?"

"Slow down, bro. No one's going to jail. I'll be okay, but listen. I need you to be really focused right now and listen to what I have to tell you. I have a couple of things that I need you to do. I'm going to New York to stay with Princess. I'm going to be supplied with a lot of work. Here's the key to my apartment, and the address. Everything is going to be there. Do not tell anyone where I'm going or take anyone to my apartment. You're in charge. As soon as I get a hold of Juice, I will let him know to give you all the money."

"But what about me? I'm running out of work," Lo interrupted. "I got my team depending on me."

"Slow down, bro. I'll get to that. First make sure that you give Juice whatever he asks for. Again, don't take anyone to the apartment."

"How am I supposed to get there?"

"We gonna go to Bike Line and get you the hottest Haro or Mongoose in the store. You're young. Police won't expect you to be doing anything. Got it?"

"Yeah, I got it."

After the talk they all took showers, got dressed, and headed to Bike Line. There were all sorts of bikes in the store. All sizes and colors. Lo picked out the hottest and most expensive bike in the store. The bike was signed by the X Games reigning champion, Dave Mirra. It was a replica of the championship bike he rode in the X Games tournament. The bike cost $2,500. Mack drove by his apartment to show Lo where it was. He then passed him two cell phones.

"One is a direct contact to me and Juice. The other phone is for you and your people. One more thing," Mack said, tossing Lo a book bag.

It felt a little heavy. Lo knew it was something good. They got out the Jeep, and Lo unloaded his bike. They entered the house and Mack wanted to kick some knowledge to his little brother before he left.

"Look, bro, I'ma be away for a while. Don't let this money get to your head. You can have it today, and tomorrow it can be all gone. So be grateful and humble. Stay out of mind and out of sight. Run things on the low. If you don't have to be in the Hole, then don't. Let your workers make money for you. Don't let no one in on what you're doing. Keep everyone guessing because once they get wind of what you're doing, they will plot and try to come for you and your shit. But niggas ain't that crazy. Trust no man or woman."

"I hear you, bro," Lo said.

"Now what's in the bag is half a key. That should be enough to hold you down for a while. Go hard for a couple of months, then chill. Plus, you'll make extra money when you grab up for Juice. I'm going to find him and let him know the situation."

All Lo was worried about was getting to the five hundred grams and chopping it up. Money was on his mind. He took in everything that Mack was telling him.

"Fall back when the work is done."

"I'm good, bro. I'll call you if I need anything."

"Aight bet," Mack said, giving Lo dap, and pulling him in for a brotherly hug. "Be safe little bro."

"Same to you."

# FIFTEEN

LO GRABBED HIS PLATE, SCALE, RAZOR, AND BAGGIES FROM under his bed. He opened up the book bag to see what a half a key looked like. The bag was filled with chunks of pieces, in all sorts of sizes. He weighed out three separate ounces. A twenty-eight for AR, Mello, and Fena. Lo already had bagged up an ounce from his previous pack, so he figured that would go to Miguel. Two hours into chopping the ounce into dubs, Lo was finally done.

After Lo dropped off the packs, he stopped into the park where everyone was drooling over his new bike. It was all chrome with royal-blue stickers that matched Dave Mirra's signature. The bike was equipped with a three-piece crank, pegs on the front, and rear wheels and a gooseneck that spun the handlebars 360 degrees. It was an exact replica.

Mello, AR, and Fena came out to the park around the same time to trap. They were blown away by the bike.

"This the type of bikes we steal," Fena said, causing everyone to laugh.

"Don't worry, we'll all have one soon," Lo replied.

~ ~ ~

Due to all the interference over the past few months, Mack was disappointed about how his plans were going. Even though Rico didn't care how long he took with his money, Mack wanted to move shit fast. He and Princess sat for hours counting money. Princess had vowed not to be involved with Mack's business, but she knew he would be with her for a couple of months, so she contributed.

Princess pulled up to Rico's rim shop with Mack in the passenger seat. Attached to the rim shop, he had a mechanic garage. As she entered, the bay doors closed behind her. She popped the trunk as Mack exited the car. She got out right behind him and sat in the waiting room. Mack pulled out the duffle bag and met Rico in his office. He placed it on top of Rico's desk.

Rico smiled as they exited the office and entered the garage, where he had a stash car prepared for him. Mack and Princess left the garage in separate cars and met at his stash house. During the ride to New York he was caught up in meditation mode. He thought to himself how exhausted he was with the fast life. The money, guns, and violence. But he was addicted to that lifestyle, and he didn't want to quit. He was sitting on money, but he knew that it wasn't enough to get his family out of the struggle.

Mack felt a little nervous leaving behind his business to Juice, but he knew it was for the better. Mack smiled as he dozed off in a light sleep thinking about his baby Princess.

BOOM! BOOM! BOOM!

Mack jumped when he heard the gunshots. His heart raced rapidly. He quickly looked at Princess wide-eyed. She noticed how scared he looked, jumping out of his sleep. She figured that he had a bad dream. Ever since he got shot and almost killed, he had multiple nightmares that woke him from his sleep.

"Hey, baby, look, we're here," she smiled. Mack looked and saw the big green sign that said Welcome to New York.

~ ~ ~

### December

During the beginning months of high school Dee, Lo's eighth-grade friend hooked him up with his cousin Jati. They were from Second Street. For the past couple of days while chilling with her, Lo and Dee spoke about business, and briefly about the south side and Second Street beef. Dee explained to Lo that here was a lot of money on Second Street and he wanted to get down with the movement. Lo was all about money and explained his reach.

He fronted Dee a half ounce, and from the first flip, Dee started buying his own work. Since Mack left, Lo spent more quality time with Jati. Mack had embedded some street smarts in Lo's brain and had explained to him that in order to last in the drug game, he had to maintain a low profile.

Most of the hustlers fuck up by buying fancy cars, big rings, and other things. All that does is attract a lot of attention from the wrong people. To succeed, you must stay off the radar. Don't show your face unless you have to. So the quality time he spent with Jati kept him out of the Hole the majority of the time. A couple of days before Lo's fourteenth birthday, he got a random text from Mello.

"I know he didn't run out of work already," he said out loud. He had used his emergency code, so Lo knew it was important. He called him immediately.

"Yo," Mello said as he answered his phone.

"It's Lo. What's good?"

"Hold up," Mello said as he passed the phone and a female's voice appeared on the line.

Lo was shocked and confused at the same time. He was thinking to himself that this couldn't be happening right now. He quickly ended the call and gave Jati a kiss goodbye without an explanation. He hopped on his bike and flew to the Hole.

Lo couldn't believe his eyes when he saw her. He hopped off his bike and grabbed hold of her. He noticed that she wasn't happy to see him. He tried to kiss her, but she moved her face.

"Jazzy, what's wrong?" Lo asked.

She immediately started to cry as she tried to speak. "How could you cheat on me and sleep with my cousin? Out of all the people, why her? I came to surprise you for your birthday, but I'm the one who got surprised."

Lo was hit with the news that he had tried to keep a secret. He couldn't believe Sandy told her, but he wasn't shocked by it.

"It was an accident, Jazzy. It only happened once. We got drunk and high, and one thing led to another." Lo tried to plead his case. He could see in her face that she was hurt. To top it off, she wanted to surprise him for his birthday. Lo felt bad. "Well you wasn't here, and I haven't heard from you in months. How was I supposed to know that we was still together?"

Lo tried to put the blame on her, but she didn't say a word.

"I can't," she said, and started walking away, leaving him where he stood.

"Jazzy!" Lo yelled. She kept walking and never looked back. He knew he had fucked up.

~ ~ ~

The crowd roared. Lo was Allentown's up-and-coming artist. He had the streets in a choke hold. His whole team was on stage with him. AR and Mello to his right, and Logan to his left. Besides Lo, Mello had a mic. Lo's dream was cut off as he was being nudged.

"Wake up, bro."

When he opened his eyes, he saw a blurry figure standing over him. As he adjusted his eyes and gained consciousness, he realized that it was Mack.

"Damn, bro, what are you doing here?" Lo asked.

"What you think? I couldn't miss my little brother's fourteenth birthday. Get up and get dressed. We have shit to do."

"Fuck, bro. It's early," Lo complained.

"Yeah. Well for starters, that's one," Mack said as he punched Lo in the shoulder.

"Aight, aight. I'm up," he replied, rubbing his shoulder. "Damn, bro, I was having this crazy dream."

"What was it?" Mack asked.

"I was performing and had the club jumping. I was a rapper, and the town loved me. They were all singing my songs."

"You sure it was you and not Husky? You know that he's the rapper in this family," Mack joked. "But anyway, are you still writing?" Lo shook his head no. "Well start writing; it might be a sign. We making money now. We can invest in some studio equipment, but until then, get your ass up. We late."

Lo got up excited for what his big brother had planned for his birthday. He took a quick shower and got dressed.

"Did you call the girl you have been seeing?" Mack asked.

"Yeah, she's waiting on us."

Mack drove down to Linden and parked up in front of Jati's house. Lo knew that Mack was about to criticize his taste, but Lo had no worries because he knew that Jati was fly. Mack blew the horn and waited for her to come out. When she walked over toward the car, Mack grinned from ear to ear.

She was stunning, and Mack complimented her instantly. Princess was not surprised. She just smiled at her future brother-in-law. Jati was light skinned and stood about five foot two. She had a slim waist and fat ass, which complimented her big brown eyes. She was shy when she entered the car but had manners and introduced herself.

Mack and Princess had plans for the young couple. Movies, mall, then dinner. After they arrived at the mall, Lo slipped $200 into Jati's clutch and told her to go shopping with Princess while he shopped with Mack. Once the two were alone, Mack spoke.

"How's business in the Hole?"

"It's moving. I took your advice and I've been on the low. I only go up there to collect my money and drop off work. I also started fucking with Jati's cousin Dee."

"Who's Dee?" Mack asked.

"Doofy Julio from Second Street," Lo said, and they both laughed.

"Oh, aight. He know about the beef?"

"Yeah. We spoke about it, but he's from Linden, part of Second."

"Just be careful with him. Have you talked to Juice?"

"Yeah, I talked to him. He been on time. Did you hear about Ricky? Word on the street, he's a rat."

"Yeah, I heard, but you know how people like to talk. Until it's in black and white, don't believe it. Just stay away from him."

"They said he set up Pretty Boy two weeks ago."

Mack was stunned. That was news to his ears, but he didn't let that affect him.

"Well we will see. Just stay away from him."

Mack went all out for Lo's birthday. He bought him three pairs of sneakers, two sweaters with matching hats, two pairs of jeans, and two jackets.

"I wanted to take you shopping in New York, but we weren't sure if Jati was allowed."

"Yeah, I don't know. Her mom be tripping on her because of me. They know that I hustle. I think they don't like me."

"She seems like a good girl, but her family comes first. So just don't give them any reason to dislike you."

"I know, but we still young, so we good for now."

"Don't you go and try to knock her up, lil bro."

"No, not at all. She's still a virgin."

"Yeah?" Mack said surprised. "Well she's a keeper."

The two brothers laughed as they approached the girls. "I see you went crazy in the stores," Lo said to Jati while looking at her bags.

"You said go shopping, so I did," Jati shot back, smiling. "Look at what we got you."

She lifted the bag toward Lo. He looked inside, and the expression on his face said it all. They waited for him to pull the gift out of the bag. When he did, he smiled from ear to ear. It was a Lawrence Taylor throwback jersey.

"It's a gift from all of us," Jati said. "We know you love your Giants."

Lo gave her a hug and kiss and thanked them all for making him so happy on his special day. Just when he thought it couldn't get any better, they had something else planned for him.

"We ain't done yet. Let's get out of here before we miss our dinner reservations," Princess said. They all headed out of the mall hugged up.

# SIXTEEN

NO ONE KNEW THAT MACK WAS IN TOWN, SO WHEN HE popped up at Jessica's house with Princess for her annual New Year's party, the entire house erupted. The place was lit. They were greeted with hugs and kisses from everyone.

"How's New York?" Juice asked Mack.

"I love it. You gotta take a week off and come visit."

"I wish I could. It's been hectic since you left. Word is out that Ricky set up Pretty Boy. Now people are scared to fuck with us. And Ricky is at war with Twelfth Street."

"Them one deuce niggas?"

"Yup. No one's fucking with him. He tried to hide up here, but I had to get rid of him. I told him shit was shut down until your legal shit was over. Speaking of that, how is everything going in court?"

"I had court early December, but they continued it. No victim, no witnesses. Two more of them and the shit gets dropped."

"That's what I'm talking about. I need you out here, cuz."

"It'll be a couple of months, but I think I got this. So how's business?" Mack said, changing the subject.

"It's good. King has been coming through heavy. He has these crazy teams of bitches who come to pick up the work for him. And Lo's been on time and consistent. I peeled him off a stack on the last run."

"That's what's up."

"If I knew that you were coming, I would have brought the tab."

"It's cool, cuz, I trust you. Enough about business tonight. Let's party and get this muthafucking place turned up."

Mack went over and grabbed a bottle of Henny out of the three cases that he had brought and started pouring shots. The DJ had the party lit. He was playing a mixture of freestyle, salsa, and hip-hop. Jessica knew how to throw a party. Everyone from the Gardens flooded the inside and outside of her house.

"Ten, nine, eight, seven, six, five, four, three, two, one, HAPPY NEW YEAR!"

The entire house erupted. Everyone went around hugging and kissing each other on the cheek. Mack was hugged up with Princess the entire time until the ball dropped. He gave her a hug and kiss and told her Happy New Year. Mack called his team together, and they surrounded him and Princess with bottles of Henny in the air. They all patiently waited for him to speak.

Lo didn't join the circle even though he was part of the team. But his loyalty was to the Hole, and Mack's entire circle was the Garde Gorillas. So Lo stood on the outside watching how Mack's team surrounded him. Mack noticed that his lil brother wasn't in his circle of family. He looked around and called out.

"Where's Lo?" Lo tried to be invisible, but that didn't work. Mack spotted him. "Come here, lil bro."

Lo walked over to where they were all gathered. Princess smiled at him. "What's up, bro?"

"Where's your glass at?" Mack asked. "Get him a glass of Henny."

One of the workers brought Lo a glass filled with liquor. Mack had a whole bottle in his hand and raised it in the air.

"To another year down that we survived. Loyalty! Honor! And the most important thing, family over everything!!!"

~ ~ ~

### The Following Night

Juice pulled a paper out of his back pocket. "Here's the count. Forty-seven. That's just from King. I told you he's been moving. We only moved five. Shit's been slow and Ricky fucked up our money. Big Poppa fell back since he took that loss when Pretty Boy got booked.

Mack's eyes turned bloodshot red. Just the thought of Ricky turning into a rat had his blood boiling.

"I ain't going back to New York. I gotta turn things around. Our money should be long by now. If Ricky's the problem, then he has to be dealt with."

Juice didn't say anything. He just gave Mack a look as if to say he had told him about Ricky. It took Mack four hours to recount the money. Even though he knew that it would be straight, he just had to take his cut out. Normally he would have waited to take his cut out, but he knew that Juice was making all the moves and didn't really profit as much as he deserved. He wanted to bless him.

Altogether Mack profited $189,000. He took $40,000 out for Juice. Mack loved him like his brother and made sure that he was good.

~ ~ ~

"Mack. What's up, papa? Long time no see."

"I'm in town. Are you around?" Mack asked.

"Yeah, I'll be in the barbershop in a half hour. See you there."

Mack knew that when Rico said a half hour, he really meant an hour. He had to figure out how he would smuggle Rico's money into the barbershop undetected. He refused to walk in, duffle bag in hand. As he drove on Union Blvd., he noticed Staples. He pulled into an empty parking space and got out. Mack walked toward the office supply section. There were computer desks, chairs, file cabinets, and other furniture. He noticed a small file cabinet sitting on the bottom shelf. It was on sale for only $15.99. He loaded it up on his cart and headed to the register.

The box was the perfect size. He emptied it out and loaded it up with money. Mack taped up the box that contained the $400,000 like it was untampered with. He walked into the barbershop, file cabinet in hand. All the barbers looked at him and laughed.

They began asking him what the box was for, but he had a quick come back. "Your boss needs it for a tax write off. You wouldn't know anything about that because it's business."

They all laughed, but Mack was the one laughing inside. His plan worked. Even Rico was confused as he saw him enter the office with a filing cabinet.

"What's up with the cabinet?"

"Let's just say it's a gift."

"You didn't have to. I got one that I don't even use."

"Well this one looks better. Just open it and tell me if you like it."

Rico untapped the box, and when he removed the plastic, he noticed that the box was filled with money. His eyes glowed.

"You know, you're a brilliant man, Mack. Who would have thought that this box contained money? I wish there were more people like you around. What's here?" Rico asked.

"That's four hundred. Put that toward the twenty-five. So we are at fifty for the coke and sixty for the weed. Shit has been slow-motion since the word got out on Ricky."

"Speaking of Ricky," Rico said as he went inside his top desk drawer and pulled out an envelope filled with a couple of papers. "Here, Mack. Read it for yourself."

"On December 6, 2020, Allentown vice met with a confidential informant *(hereafter)* discussing drug activities of Matt "Pretty Boy" Mendez. CI contacted Mendez at 610-407-2104 via cellphone for *(28)* twenty-eight grams of crack cocaine. CI met with Mendez at Nineth and Gordon where the transaction was observed. Detectives performed a field test of a sample and obtained a positive result.

Mack was speechless. He had the proof that he needed.

"Mack, we had a chance to kill him and his family, but you had told me that you would take care of it. So I took your word."

Mack interrupted. "I know what I said, and I'ma take care of it."

"Just make sure you do things smart. If you need my team, just ask."

"Say no more. Thanks!"

Mack was furious. He placed the paperwork in his pocket and walked out of Rico's office. Not only did Ricky shoot him, but he also dropped word on everyone, then he set up Pretty Boy. Mack rushed to his house trying to get his mind right. He sat on his mother's sofa speechless.

He didn't want to lay his best friend down, but he knew that he had to. He wouldn't let anyone else do it. His eyes got watery at the thought of killing Ricky. Suddenly his thoughts were interrupted.

Princess was trying to seduce Mack by kissing him on his neck as she leaned over him from behind. She felt the tension and eased off.

"What's wrong?" she asked.

"Nothing, babe. Just a lot of shit on my mind."

"Is everything okay?"

"Yes, but I think I'ma have to stay down here for a while. I got some things I gotta take care of."

"I understand, babe. Lo left you a note. He said to read it once you get in."

Mack read the note and headed to Lo's room. He followed Lo's instructions and revealed the hidden treasure. Through all the bullshit, he had managed to make Mack's day. Wrapped up in a black bag was $12,000 for a half a brick. Mack passed Princess the money and told her to put it in the safe. Then he gave her a kiss and whispered in her ear.

"Get ready. We're going to Jessica's."

# SEVENTEEN

IT'D BEEN A WHILE SINCE LO STEPPED INTO THE HOLE. EVEN with his absence he still made money. He brought out a pack of twenty dubs that were worth $400. Once he got to the park, he walked directly to Logan's house. Logan stepped out of his crib with his basketball in hand.

The park was packed. Even with the blistering cold, everybody was still out. Lo wore his jacket with a hoody underneath. Once the sun dropped, money started to flow in. Him, AR, Mello, Logan, and a couple of the old heads posted up at the money tree. They all took turns serving fiends. Mello was the first person to spot the speeding car shooting down Bradford. Then another one shot up Turner.

"Five-O, jump out," he yelled.

Everyone started running in different directions. The cars stopped simultaneously, and three white dudes from each car jumped out pointing their guns and screaming.

"Freeze! Get on the fucking ground."

No one paid them any attention as they continued running. Once they reached the park, Logan and AR ran in the direction of Logan's house. Mello and Lo ran through the park toward Mello's house. They leaped onto the step wall and ran across it. Lo pulled out the dubs he had left and closed them in the grass. When he looked back, Mello was trailing as he noticed vice tackling one of the old heads.

"Mello, keep up. We about to hop off and hit the woods," Lo yelled.

Him and Mello hit the woods winded. There were no cops in sight. They stood there for an hour, until they felt like the coast was clear. That was the first time that they were caught in a raid. Lo and Mello left the woods and headed back to the park. They were hoping that Logan and AR didn't get snatched up. Lo knocked on Logan's door, and his mom answered.

"Hey, Joanna, is Logan home?" Lo asked as he heard her phone ring. "No, he hasn't got in yet. Hold on, let me get my phone," she said. Two minutes later she returned with a hysterical look on her face. "That was the cops. Logan got arrested. I have to go pick him up. I'll tell him that you was here."

"It's okay, Joanna. We'll wait," Mello said.

"Fuck! I hope AR didn't have anything on him," Lo said.

"Nah, I doubt it," replied Mello.

Lo and Mello waited outside until they saw Logan's dad's car pulling up. He got out of the car with a smile on his face.

"What happened with AR?" That was the first question Lo had for him once they started talking.

"He's good. He just had to wait for his mom to come pick him up. They booked Tapp and old head Charles, though. They both served vice."

"Damn, that could have been us," Lo said. "But since we are all good, I'ma head out."

Lo dapped up his team and headed to the back of Mello's crib to retrieve his work. He was breaking his head trying to figure out who they served that was vice. He thought about the bitch that was in the white Chevy, because she looked funny.

~ ~ ~

Mack stopped at Isabel's house searching for Ricky. It wasn't any surprise that he wasn't home. Isabel said that she hadn't seen him in weeks. The last time she saw him was two weeks before Christmas. He didn't even have the courtesy to call her during the holidays. She broke down all the information Mack needed to find Ricky.

Isabel said that he'd been staying with big booty Kathy from Penbrook. Mack noticed that the house was messy, so he reached into his pockets and flipped out $400 and gave it to Isabel. He gave her a kiss on the cheek and thanked her for the information. Mack hoped in his Jeep and headed toward the Brook. The Brook was dead, not a single soul in sight. It was cold out, but that shouldn't stop a hustler from making money.

Mack pulled up on Livingston Street, where Kathy lived. Outside her house sat three crates and a kitchen chair. On the side of the house was a lot of trash, as if no one had cleaned up in a while. Mack walked up to the door and knocked. After two minutes of him knocking, Kathy came to the door. A strong odor hit Mack's nostrils. It was a smell that he was familiar with. Trying not to throw up, he spoke.

"Hey, Kathy."

"What's up, Mack?" Kathy said, surprised. "What are you doing here?"

"I'm looking for Ricky. Is he here?"

"Yeah, he's upstairs. Let me get him. Don't mind the mess."

Mack was familiar with Kathy. When Juice was adopted by his Bethlehem foster family, he introduced Mack to Kathy. They had kicked it for a little, and he wasn't surprised that Ricky was fucking her. But what really surprised him was the smell of crack coming from her house. He peaked his head inside, where he saw the stems and paraphernalia lying on the living room table.

Mack knew that Ricky was on that shit, but Kathy too? That was the biggest surprise of all. When Ricky saw Mack, he smiled from ear to ear.

"Mack, my brother. What's up?" he said, giving him a hug. "Where the fuck you been?"

"I've been around since Lo's birthday. Where the fuck you been?"

"I've been out here in the Brook trying to get this money. Ever since Pretty Boy sold to vice, I've been on the low."

"Pretty Boy's locked up?" Mack asked as if he didn't know.

Ricky gave Mack the rundown on how Pretty Boy was set up by crackhead Bob. Mack knew that he was frauding, but continued to let him talk.

"What's good with that?" Mack asked, pointing to the

stem and paraphernalia on the table. Ricky followed Mack's fingers over to the stems. Ricky's face turned beet red. He was embarrassed. Mack yelled at him. "You still on that shit?"

Ricky put his head down as if Mack was scolding him. "I can't kick the habit. I tried," Ricky admitted as tears came to his eyes.

"It's okay, I got you," Mack said as he embraced him. "Look, go up and get cleaned up. Here's my new number. Give me a call when you're done, so we can talk."

Ricky smiled. "Aight, bro. Give me about an hour."

Mack left Ricky feeling a little sorrow. He knew he had to lay him down. Ricky was bad for business. It would only be a matter of time before he tried to set up one of Mack's people. He wasn't having that. Mack drove the long way to his hood.

He thought long and hard about how he was going to kill Ricky. He knew that Ricky would be holding and wouldn't go down easy. Stress was creeping on Mack's face. He needed a stress reliever. Mack pulled out his cell phone and called Juice.

"Yo, cuz," Juice said.

"Cuz, where are you at?"

"Jessica's. You coming up?"

"On my way. You got weed?"

"Is a fat bitch heavy?" Juice replied as the cousins busted out laughing.

"Juice, you're fucking crazy. I'm on my way."

~ ~ ~

"Lo, Lo, Lo!" the crowd was screaming his name. When he stepped on the stage the crowd went crazy. Lo looked back as he was followed by Logan and Mello. He looked into the crowd as they chanted his name. He glanced at the DJ and gave him a head nod to play the beat. The beat roared through the speakers. The crowd went bananas. As Lo lifted his arm up to speak into the mic, his vision was interrupted. He noticed this beautiful Puerto Rican in the crowd. From where he stood, she looked to be about five feet tall.

She was light skinned with jet-black curly hair. He was so caught up on her that he didn't realize that his song was playing. Luckily his voices were on the track. Before he could catch up to his verse, his dream was interrupted by a wet kiss. His eyes opened slowly.

"Jati, is that you?" he said, confused. He saw a blurry vision, a silhouette of a female.

"Wake up, sleepyhead," Jati said as she kissed him again.

"What are you doing here?"

"I came to get you. I missed you."

"I missed you too. I just had the craziest dream."

"What were you dreaming about?"

"I was performing."

"Performing?" Jati asked, looking confused.

"Yeah. That's the second dream I had like that."

"You sure it wasn't Husky? You know he's the rapper. Speaking of Husky, you know he's talking to my sister, right? They were chilling last night."

"Who, Kelly?"

"Yup, and where was you?"

"You know that I was in the Hole making money."

"Yeah. Now you don't got time for me?" Jati said, making a sad face.

"Stop talking shit. You know I love you," Lo replied as

he tried to give her a kiss.

"Yuck!" Jati screamed. "Go brush your teeth with your afternoon breath."

"Shut up and get over here," Lo said as he pulled her close to him. "You know I love you, right?"

"Yes, Lo. You know I love you too. Now go get dressed."

Lo got up with an erection clear as day, bulging out of his boxers. "Look at what you did," he said, looking down at his pipe. Jati smiled.

"I see I got that effect on you," she replied, getting up and walking over to Lo. She grabbed his dick and rubbed it gently. "Don't worry, when the time is right, I'll take care of it. Now go take a shower."

Lo smiled. He knew she was a virgin, and he didn't want to rush her into having sex. He really loved her.

"You better, you tease. Get me out some clothes," Lo said as he went to take a shower.

Ever since Mack got shot, he moved his family to a different location. Lo felt extremely comfortable with the move because the east side was all his. He and Jati walked hand in hand down Hanover Avenue, not caring about anything. If you didn't know them, they looked like the perfect couple, two lovebirds enjoying life. As different cars sped down the block, they pointed to their future cars.

"Navigator. That's mine," Jati said as the SUV flew by.

"Range Rover," Lo replied. He could spot them from a mile away.

"Porsche," Jati said as the coupe sped through the light.

"A two-seater?" Lo said. "How are we going to fit the kids in that?"

"Kids?" she asked, surprised.

"What, you don't want to have kids?"

"Lo, I would love to have your kids."

"So then, we are going to need one of these," Lo said, pointing to a minivan that cruised past.

The two lovebirds laughed. They gossiped about life as they walked to her Linden Street home. When Jati and Lo arrived, her mom was cooking dinner. She made yellow rice with beans, pork chops, and a salad on the side. Lo hadn't eaten a home-cooked meal in years. He was so busy in the streets ripping and running all day long that he never worried about it.

After dinner they sat on her porch steps and watched the weekend traffic drive by. It was a cold and breezy night. Lo wrapped his arms around her as she sat between his legs, trying to keep her warm. He kissed her on top of her head and closed his eyes. He was in bliss.

# EIGHTEEN

DURING MACK'S VISIT WITH RICKY, THINGS WERE BITTER-
sweet. You felt the distance between them. The tension
was there, but the two killers didn't budge. Ricky wasn't
sure if Mack really knew about Pretty Boy, because the
penalty would be death, but he wasn't going to blow his
cover.

After Ricky got ready, he called Mack to meet up, but
Mack called the meeting off. He was testing Ricky to see
if he would really call. When he did, Mack told him that he
had a business meeting, stalling their hookup.

It was a Sunday afternoon when Mack hopped out of
the shower. This was the day that he planned to say
goodbye to his right-hand man forever. The night before,
Mack couldn't sleep. He tossed and turned for hours.
Mack was never afraid to kill, but for some reason this kill
didn't feel right with him.

Each time he closed his eyes, he was reminded about
his past: the day he met Ricky outside his mother's house,
and all their football games they played together. Growing
up they were inseparable. Mack sat on his bed after he

finished getting dressed, holding his Desert Eagle in his hand. He spoke softly to himself.

"Why, Ricky? Why the fuck did you put me in this situation?"

He released the clip and took the bullet out of the chamber. The clip was fully loaded. Mack grabbed his blue handkerchief, wiped the single bullet, and reloaded it into the clip. He slapped the clip back in and cocked it.

**8 Hours Later**

"Mack, where you at? I'm here."

"I'm on the bridge heading toward you."

Mack was nervous. He'd been circling around the spot for the past ten minutes. You could tell he didn't want to kill Ricky, but he had to. That was the only way to make things right. He finally parked the car and waited a few minutes before exiting. His hands were sweating, not because he was about to commit murder, because the target was his right-hand man.

"Time to get this over with," Mack said, trying to encourage himself.

He took a look back to make sure no one was following him. The last time he stepped foot in their secret location was when Ricky was shot. Heat came over his body when he thought about Ricky accidentally shooting him trying to kill Rico. Then his state changed: Mack entered the stash house mad.

"Ricky!" Mack yelled in the not-so-empty apartment.

"I'm right here," Ricky said as he exited the bedroom.

"What you doing in there?"

"Nothing, just thinking. Thinking how much has changed since we were young. It was always you and me. Now that we've gotten older, it seems like money got between us."

"Money ain't get between us, Ricky. Drugs got the best of you. Haven't you noticed?"

"I ain't change, Mack, you did," Ricky yelled. "Look at you. You look like money, while me, your right-hand man, looks like a fiend."

"Ricky, I tried to get you help. You didn't want it."

"I don't need it. I can control the urge." Ricky began to weep as he stared into Mack's eyes.

Mack wasn't sure if Ricky knew what was coming to

him. Or did he, and he was trying to plead his case? "Look, Ricky," Mack said.

Ricky interrupted. "No, you fucking look," he yelled as he pulled out his twin Desert Eagle. "What you got us here for? What are you trying to do? I know you didn't call us here to talk."

Mack instantly pulled out his gun. It was identical to Ricky's. "Ricky, put that gun away."

"What you think, I wasn't onto you? I know you called us here so you could kill me! I know you. I know all about you. I know you know about Pretty Boy," Ricky stated as tears came down his eyes, still clutching his gun.

Mack didn't say a word. He wasn't surprised that Ricky was on point, but he didn't show his cards. "Why, Pretty? Why did you set him up?"

"'Cause that pussy got me hooked to this shit," Ricky yelled, swinging his arms all over the place.

"You should have killed him. We live by the code of the streets, and you know what happens to rats," Mack said as he raised his gun, catching Ricky slipping.

Ricky's eyes widened as Mack raised his weapon. He knew he had the jump on him. He dropped his gun to the floor and began crying, showing a sign of defeat.

"Go ahead, Mack, do what you came here to do. Just know that I would have never took you down. Look into my eyes when you pull the trigger, because I would never let anyone other than you kill me," he told Mack as tears came down his face.

Mack's eyes watered up as he aimed his gun at his best friend. "I'm sorry, Ricky. Just know that I love you, and I will take care of your family for as long as I live."

Ricky looked him dead in his eyes. Mack could see that he had no soul. Mack squeezed the trigger.

BOOM!

The blast echoed through the apartment. The impact from the .50 cal blew half of his face off. Blood splattered everywhere as his body dropped. Tears continued to fall from Mack's eyes as he dropped down to his knees.

"I'm sorry," Mack said as he grabbed his best friend's lifeless body.

Mack started searching his pockets to make sure he didn't leave any evidence. He picked up both guns and left the apartment. He ran to his car, popped the trunk, and retrieved a gas can filled with gasoline. He jogged back to the apartment, spread gas throughout the place, then lit a match as he opened the door.

"See you on the other side." He threw the match, and the entire room engulfed in flames.

"Breaking news: A fire erupted just after 9:00 p.m. on the 1100 block of South Gilmore Street. Police found a body burned to death. They have no leads as to the gender or identity of this person at this time. Detectives found traces of blood splattered on the front door. Anyone with information is to contact the Allentown police detectives."

"Damn, someone wanted that person dead," Juice said as he watched the weekend news with Mack. "'Cuz, you see that shit?"

Mack didn't respond. His facial expression said it all.

"What's up, bro? You aight?" Juice asked.

Mack looked up as tears came to his eyes. "That's Ricky. I killed him."

Juice took his eyes off the TV and looked at Mack. "You did what?"

"I killed him, cuz. He had to go."

"Damn, cuz. Anyone see you?"

"No, I'm good, but how am I gonna tell Isabel about this?"

"You ain't gonna say shit. Once the police identify the body, they will contact her, then she will contact you. So remain as if you don't know shit," Juice said.

~ ~ ~

BOOM! BOOM! BOOM! BOOM

"Who the fuck is it now?" Isabel spoke out loud as she headed to the front door. As she opened it, in front of her were two men dressed in suits.

"Hello, Isabel. My name is Detective Smith, and this is my partner Detective Russell. Do you mind if we step inside?"

"What the fuck did Ricky do now?" she asked as she stepped to the side and let them in.

"We are investigating a homicide."

"A homicide?" Izzy interrupted. "Who did my son kill?"

"Ricky didn't kill anyone. Is your son named Ricardo Sanchez?"

She thought about it for a moment. If Ricky didn't kill anyone, why are they here? "Yes, that's my son."

"We have reason to believe that Ricky has been killed," Det. Smith said.

Isabel lost it. "No, no, no, no, not my baby. Who killed him?"

"We don't know, Isabel. That why we are here. We're trying to find out."

Det. Russell spoke, "Look, Isabel, we found his body in a vacant apartment located on the south side. Do you know who owns that apartment?"

"No. Can I see my son?"

"I'm sorry, ma'am, he's been severely burned. We have nearly no remains left of him."

"So how do you know that that's my son?" she asked, puzzled.

"There were traces of blood splattered on the living room door that matched Ricky's. From the angle of the blood splatter, we believe he was shot."

Isabel began to cry again. "My baby. I told him."

"Ma'am, do you know if Ricky had any recent problems with anybody?"

"No, officer. My son didn't have any problems with

anybody. Now if you'll excuse me, I need to start getting ready to prepare my son's funeral."

"Yes ma'am. Here's my card. If you hear anything that you would like to share with us, give me a call."

Isabel grabbed the card out of his grasp. "I sure would," she said sarcastically. Once the officers were gone, she jumped on her cell phone and called Mack.

~ ~ ~

It was a sad day at Johnson's Funeral Home. Izzy contained herself, knowing the lifestyle Ricky lived. She knew that death came with the territory. Mack knew that Izzy would be going through a lot, so he and Jessica planned out his funeral. Ricky's body was severely burned, so he had to be cremated. Mack bought Izzy a 24-karat gold urn for his remains. He wanted to make sure that he went out in style.

The funeral was packed with mourners. Besides his mutual family, members from the Gardens and the Hole attended. Rumors had been spreading fast about who was responsible for Ricky's death. Word on the street, Pretty Boy was responsible since he'd been in MIA since he bailed out of prison.

"Mack," Lo whispered.

"What's up, lil bro?"

"Pretty Boy got Ricky killed?" Lo said as tears came down in the hallway.

"I don't know, bro. But don't worry about it. I'll take care of it."

"Okay," Lo said as he continued crying.

Mack got up and sat next to Isabel and gave her a compassionate hug and kiss. "Hey, ma. How are you doing?"

"I'm okay, Mack."

Mack reached inside his pocket and pulled out a key. He passed it to Isabel and said, "Here, ma. A new key to your new life."

Mack knew the memories alone would haunt her. She cried some more then thanked Mack before speaking to the crowd.

After she spoke on behalf of her son, she pulled Mack to the side. "When you find out they killed my son?"

"I'ma kill him."

"No, Mack. I don't want another mother going through what I'm going through. So, for me, give him a pass."

"I don't know if I can do that."

"You have to promise me," Isabel said.

Mack looked into Izzy's eyes and knew that she was serious. Before he got up, he kissed her on her cheek and whispered.

"I promise."

~ ~ ~

**2 Months Later**

"District Attorney Malarki, where are your witnesses and the victim?" Judge Stevens asked.

"They are not present at this time. Your Honor, Mr. Ortiz is a very powerful man. The witnesses and victims are being threatened not to come to court."

Mack kept his poker face on as the DA was furious that his witnesses didn't show up to testify against him.

"Your Honor, that's frivolous," Rossi yelled.

"That's enough, Malarki. This case has been going on for too long. When it comes to the Commonwealth versus Mack Ortiz, one count of attempted murder, we have no choice but to dismiss and drop all charges."

The courtroom erupted as Mack smiled and hugged his high-profile attorney.

"Thank you, Mr. Rossi. I knew you would get me out of this tight situation."

"No problem, Mack. You just make sure you keep yourself out of trouble."

Mack released his grip from his lawyer and turned around to his girlfriend, who was sitting in the front row.

"We did it," Princess said as she hugged Mack out of the courtroom.

"No, you did it, love. Thank you."

"Anything for my baby," she replied.

"Hey, Rossi," Mack yelled in the courtroom hallway. "Lunch on me." Rossi smiled as the powerful trio left the courthouse.

# NINETEEN

EVER SINCE MACK GOT BACK, BUSINESS HAD BEEN GOING good. Lo was the flyest ninth grader in school. His freshman year was coming to an end. He sat in his seventh-period class thinking about how his summer was going to be. In the past year, he lost a few of his homies to the streets, and he thought the summer would be turned up for more homicides. At that moment, Lo caught a glimpse of his two classmates talking about him.

"What's up, Yen and Janet? What are y'all laughing and talking about?"

Janet's face sizzled up as she was caught red-handed. "My friend likes you," Yen said. "She thinks you're hot."

Lo smiled at her compliment. "Does she? So why don't she speak for herself?" he asked.

Lo knew of Janet since eighth grade. She was very pretty and an intelligent female. She stood at five foot one, with shoulder-length blonde hair. Her eyes were olive green, and she had a cheerleader body.

"She's shy," Yen replied.

Lo knew that she was shy. He could tell because she barely spoke to anyone in class. He grabbed his pen, tore off a piece of his writing paper, and jotted down his cell phone number, then slid it to Janet.

"Here's my number. Call me when you have time."

Janet's cheeks were burning red as she looked embarrassed and happy at the same time. She grabbed the number and placed it in her pocket.

"I'll call you tonight, if that's okay."

"Yeah, that's cool. The sooner, the better," he said, winking his eye as the school bell rang.

The entire classroom rose up as each student tried to exit the room. Once Lo got into the hallway, he noticed Janet and Yen posted up by the lockers. They made eye contact as he got closer. He smiled. Janet started walking in his direction, which made Lo freeze as he analyzed her beautiful frame. She walked up to Lo and kissed him on the lips, then spun around before he could kiss her back. She took a glimpse back; Lo was still in shock. "I'll call you," she said and walked off.

Lo smiled. He didn't see that coming. He left the school and met up with his team at the baseball stoops.

"What you cheesing about?" asked Frisk as Lo gave him dap.

"Remember white girl Janet?"

"Yen's friend?"

"Yeah. Just snatched her up. Gave her my number, then shorty snuck a kiss and walked off. She left me hanging."

"Word. See what's up with Yen for me. Besides that, let's roll. We got shit to do."

~ ~ ~

Lo kicked off his sneakers and placed them in their box. It was a long day in the Hole. In his pockets were crumpled up bills. Normally he didn't serve fiends, but the Hole was jumping. He giggled to himself as he found a bag of weed in between his bilks. Lo placed his phones on top of his dresser and headed to Husky's room. He called out to him.

"Husky, are you there?"

There was no answer, so he opened the bedroom door. The room was dark. Lo flicked on the light switch and scanned the room. He headed toward his drawers in search of a dutch. He ransacked each drawer until he located a box of dutches. There was one left inside.

"Lucky me," he said as he snatched it up.

When he made it back to his room, he noticed his cell phone vibrating. He grabbed his phone and saw that he had three missed calls. The number was unfamiliar to his eyes, so he called back instantly.

"Hello," the beautiful voice shot through the phone, making Lo's insides start to quiver.

He knew exactly who it was, but he played dumb. "Did someone just call me from there?"

"Yes, Lo, it's me, Janet."

Lo laughed when she said who it was. The two spoke for hours of their likes and dislikes and why neither of them spoke to each other during school. Janet was polite and was raised with manners. She was everything Lo wanted in a girlfriend. Even though they were raised differently from each other, he was feeling her. It was about 2:00 a.m., and Lo was still talking to Janet when he heard a bang on his front door.

"Fuck the police." The line went dead.

~ ~ ~

It was a hot sunny day, and everyone was out in the

Gardens. School was over, and the block was jumping. Mack and Junito were posted up at the mailboxes, while Husky and Vic patrolled the first parking lot. Juice had a dutch in his hand, smoking, when a blue Honda pulled up with four females inside asking for weed. Juice asked what they wanted, and the passenger told him five dimes. He walked behind a parked car and grabbed his stash on the rear tire and grabbed five dimes. As Juice approached the car, he decided that he was going to spit some game.

"Hey, ma, what's your name?"

"I'm Veronica. That's Nicky, Susan, and the driver is my sis Tonya."

"Okay. How about I give you my number so next time you want some smoke, you can just call me. You don't have to come out here; this shit is too hot. Plus, if you want to chill, we can do that too."

Veronica took a long look at Juice and his squad, as they looked like money, then spoke. "How about we chill now?"

"I don't see that being a problem," Juice replied.

The four pretty females hopped out of the car and posted up with the fellas. Juice introduced the ladies to the rest of the team.

"Do you wanna smoke?" Veronica asked.

Juice laughed as if it was a funny question. "Here's some dutches. Do you know how to roll?" he asked as he held them out to her.

She grabbed them from his hand and went to work. She unwrapped the dutch like a pro. Juice noticed she was a tease because every time she licked the dutch, she looked at Juice seductively.

After smoking with the females, the trio decided to grab some grub from McDonald's on South Fourth Street. When they pulled up to the drive-thru, they noticed the nigga Mark with a couple of the Second Street niggas.

"You trying to smoke these niggas now?" Junito spurted out. He was a live wire and was always prepared to let his gun clap.

Mack was caught up between beef and money. He knew the rules. You can't make money and beef at the same time. During his departure to New York, Mark and his squad tried to run down on Junito and the lil homies in the Gardens. He knew Junito wanted to let his cannon go, and Mack didn't want to be the one to stop him.

"Yeah, my nigga, let's ride on these bitch-ass niggas."

~ ~ ~

"Don't look, but that looks like Mack and them Gorilla niggas pulling up," said Mark.

"I told you we shouldn't have came to this McDonald's," Chiki said.

"Man, them niggas ain't gonna dictate where I eat," Mark shouted.

"Yeah, fuck them niggas," Tommy said.

"It's cool, Chiki. I'ma hit up Paco."

Paco loaded up his chopper with the hundred-round clip and hopped in his Astro van. As he pulled up to the McDonald's, he noticed that Mack's car was parked up inside the old Kmart shopping center, just how Mark had explained. Paco inched closer to Mack's car and noticed that nobody was inside.

"Decoy," Paco said out loud. He quickly scanned the parking lot to see if Mack had the drop on him. He made a quick U-turn and headed back toward McDonald's.

Mark saw Paco pull up and headed toward Mack's car. He smiled and anticipated death as he stared at Mack's car. He then noticed Paco drive past and then pop a U-turn. Mark was confused. He wondered why he didn't shoot. Then his phone rang.

"Yo, where they at?"

"You passed the car."

"No one is in it."

"No one is in it?" Mark repeated.

Chiki just shook his head. Mark quickly exited the McDonald's with his crew trailing him. Paco pulled up to Mark and told him he'd follow them out.

~ ~ ~

"Ain't that Paco in that Astro van?" Kamikaze asked.

"Yeah, that's that nigga. They must have seen us pulling in," Mack replied.

Mack knew the art of war. He was always a step ahead of the game. He had a feeling Mark spotted him, so he quickly called up Kamikaze to scoop them up in a rental.

"Kazi, once they pull out, pull up on the side of the whip and I'ma let them have it," Junito said.

Kamikaze did just as he was told. He was Mack's protégé. Mack has been molding him since he was thirteen years old. If you didn't know Kazi well, you could have easily mistaken him for Mack's little brother Lo.

Junito slid the van door open and let off three shots into

the Astro van. The shots caught Paco off guard as he slammed his foot on the gas pedal, then rear-ended Mark's car. Junito chuckled in the backseat as Kazi rushed to the Gardens.

~ ~ ~

"Any of you hit?" Mark asked.

"Nah, we good," Chiki and Tommy said simultaneously.

Mark hopped on his jack and called Paco.

"Yo, they crept up on us. Any of you hit?" Paco asked as he trailed Mark.

"No, we good. Listen, meet on the block. We going hunting."

Mark, Chiki, Tommy, and Paco hopped inside their buddy's black Caravan. This time they were ready for war as they headed to the south side. The entire van was on mute as they entered the Gardens. They felt like if the Gorillas were there, they were on point. There wasn't a soul in sight. All of a sudden Mark's phone went off.

"Yo," Mark said as he answered the call. "Oh yeah. Are you sure? Say no more, on my way." He ended the call. "I just got a call. Mack's about to hit up the Hole. Let's ride over there and catch that pussy slipping."

As the Caravan approached the entrance to the Hole,

they noticed Mack was also pulling in. Paco played it cool as he made a smooth left into the projects. Mack didn't even look his way. Paco followed him all the way out of the Hole, onto Hanover Avenue.

"Where are we gonna let him have it?" Tommy asked.

"Wait a little. I want to get him good," Mark replied.

The Caravan followed Mack past the Woody's, then the 7-Eleven, then on Maxwell Street where he had made a left. Once Mack hit the stop sign, Mark let it rip.

POP! POP! POP! POP! POP! POP! POP!

~ ~ ~

After the shootout on the south side, Mack got scooped up by one of his buddies, where he rented his black Ford Explorer. He got a call from O, a hustler from the Hole, for 250 grams. It seemed a little funny to Mack due to the time, but he knew O was not that stupid. Before making the sale, Mack took a quick drive through. As he approached the intersection to the Hole, he noticed a funny dark Caravan about to turn into the Hole. He knew they were known to have vice in them, so he slowly crept up East Linden Street, made a right on Bradford, and exited the Hole.

The van trailed him. Mack was on ice. No drugs, no gun,

so he was clean. He made a left on Hanover Avenue, as the van kept their distance. He passed the Woody's doing the speed limit. He saw the Hess and thought about pulling in, but there was too much traffic, so he kept it pushing.

Once he hit Maxwell Street, he banged a left. The Caravan made the same left, and Mack chuckled. As he approached the stop sign, he slowed down. As he was making the stop, he looked through his rearview mirror and noticed the speeding van coming toward him with the passenger window down. He noticed the long barrel from an AK-47 extend from the window.

POP! POP! POP! POP! POP! POP! POP!

The sound of the AK infuriated Mack. He punched the gas pedal, swerving side to side, trying to dodge the bullets. He could hear the bullets penetrating the metal of the truck. Each time he turned the corner, the shooters let off more shots. Mack knew the east side; it was his second home. So he dipped into the narrow alleys until he lost the shooters. He pulled up to the driveway of his eastside house at full speed. He hopped out of the riddled truck, ran in the house, and slammed it shut.

~ ~ ~

"Damn."

Lo was shaken by the loud bang on the door. He immediately hung up on Janet thinking it was a raid. He slowly walked toward his bedroom door, where he was met by Mack.

"Mack, you scared the shit out of me."

"Lo, go downstairs and look out the window. Let me know if you see a dark Caravan driving around. Niggas tried to kill me."

Lo didn't hesitate. He ran to the living room window and looked out for Mack. Mack came down the steps dressed in all black, carrying a Jansport book bag. Lo knew he was going to war with whoever just tried to park him. He also knew what was inside the bag. There was a full arsenal in that book bag. Mack was speechless as he opened the door.

"Mack, be careful," Lo said as his brother disappeared through the door.

# TWENTY

LO WOKE UP THE FOLLOWING MORNING ON HIS MOTHER'S sofa. He headed toward Mack's room looking for him. He hadn't returned. Lo grabbed his phone to check the time and to see if he had any missed calls. He had five of them. Before checking the missed calls, he turned on the television to the 69 news at noon. While the news ran, he checked his call log. He noticed that Jati and Janet had called him. He had two voice messages and pressed the call button.

"Hey Lo, it's Janet. Just wanted to make sure everything was okay with you. You hung up last night very quickly. Call me when you get time."

Lo quickly deleted the message, and it automatically went to the next voice message.

"HI, baby. It's your girl. Did you forget you had one? Call me, I want to see you."

Lo hung up his phone and focused on the news. Nothing excited him, so he jumped in the shower. A half hour later, he stepped out of his house where the summer sun beamed on him. He was fresh to death. He pulled out his phone and called Janet. She answered on the first ring.

"What happened to you last night? You just hung up. I tried to call you back, but you didn't answer."

"I'm sorry. Something happened and I had to step out, and I forgot to take my phone with me."

"Are you okay?"

Lo was surprised how concerned she was. He wasn't used to that coming from a female. Any other chick would have flipped out, but not Janet. She was special.

"Yeah, I'm okay."

"Okay. Look, me and my friends are going to the movies tonight. I would like it if you could meet me there. I want to spend some time with you."

"Let me handle a few things and I'll call you in a couple of hours and let you know."

Janet agreed as they said their goodbyes. Lo walked through the streets of the east side as he headed to the Hole, getting his thoughts together. Ever since he started making money, he lost focus on school and football. He wasn't sure if they were a priority anymore. They say once you get a taste of that life, it's hard to get out of. Besides the money, the war between the south side and Second Street was getting crazy. Even though Lo repped the east side, it didn't matter, because his brother was a diehard southsider and he was blood.

Lo knew he had to stay on point because if they couldn't get Mack, they would come for him. He strolled through eastside alleys trying to avoid main streets because he wasn't strapped. Once he entered the Hole, he knew he was safe.

Logan was in the park shooting around while the old heads sat on the wall cyphering a few dutches. Lo dapped the squad before jumping on the court with Logan.

"What's good? Where is all the niggas at?" Lo asked, referring to the young boys.

"I don't know. I've been out here all day. I haven't seen anybody yet."

"Any fiends come through?"

"No, shit's been slow. Hit Cutthroat. See if you can catch a few."

"You trying to eat?" Lo asked.

"Hell yeah," Logan responded in a heartbeat.

~ ~ ~

"Let me get two cheeseburgers, everything on it, and two orders of fries," Lo said to his personal chef Olga. He then walked outside.

Lo and Logan grabbed two crates and sat outside of George's waiting for the food and some fiends. Lo had brought out ten dubs to make a quick dollar. During the past six months, his profit went up and down. He blew the majority of it on clothes, food, and other things for him and the team. He made sure everyone ate, even the ones that didn't hustle.

At fourteen years old, Lo had run through twenty thousand dollars, with just a bunch of wardrobes to show for it. He figured as long as he had Mack to rely on, he could blow money and come back up. George came out with the food and two iced teas on two Styrofoam trays. As Lo ate, he was watching his surroundings.

He noticed that Mack drove up East Linden Street with another car trailing him. From afar it looked like it was Juice. He didn't say a word. He looked at Logan as he was chomping away on his burger. The two finished their food, then headed back to the park.

They walked up East Linden Street. Once they got to the yellow poles, they noticed that the park was packed.

Sandy and Kim were sitting on their stoop as Lo and Logan approached. Lo said hi and gave Sandy a flirty look. She giggled and just said hi in return. As they headed to the park, Lo noticed that Mack had spotted him and started walking toward him.

"Mack, what's up? You aight?" Lo asked.

"Yeah, I'm good. I need to talk to you."

Logan walked off and left the brothers alone to talk.

"Lo, shit just got real. I need you to take this and wear it at all times," Mack said as he took off his shirt, unstrapping his Kevlar vest.

"Mack, it's too hot for that shit," Lo complained.

"I don't give a fuck. You better keep this shit on. I don't trust these niggas up here, and you shouldn't either."

He looked around and noticed every nigga from the Hole was watching Mack shelter him with the vest and placed it over his wifebeater.

"Make sure you keep your shirt on. I'll let you know when it's safe to take it off."

"Bro, but what's going on?" Lo asked, concerned.

"Niggas tried to kill me yesterday, and I was told that

these hole niggas are riding with them Second Street niggas."

Lo instantly got angry as Mack broke the news about his niggas, the same niggas that he thought were loyal to him. "Say no more, bro. I'll keep my eyes and ears open."

Mack gave him dap and a hug. Before Lo let Mack leave, he spoke.

"Are you going to be busy around six? My shorty wants me to meet her at the movies, but I need a ride."

"I got you, bro. Meet me at the house at 5:30."

~ ~ ~

"Here, bro, your ticket. Enjoy the movie. Call me twenty minutes before you're ready to leave, and I'll be here."

Lo grabbed his ticket and walked through the theatre doors looking fresh to death as usual. Janet spotted him and called him over toward her and her friends. Yen and Kayla were speaking to Janet and giggled as Lo got close. He knew they were talking about him.

"Hey, Lo, you look nice today," Janet said.

"Thanks," he replied as he gave her a soft kiss. "You look beautiful as well."

She grabbed him by the hand and led him to the theatre room. Once the movie started, she cuddled under his arm. She laid her head on his chest, and he squeezed her closer by her shoulders.

"I can see myself with her for a long time," Lo thought to himself. He gently kissed her on top of her hair, inhaling her exotic scent. She lifted her head and gazed into his eyes. She puckered up her lips, and he leaned in for a kiss.

"Do you see yourself being with me for a long time?" Lo asked Janet.

"I do, Lo. I had my eyes on you for so long. I would like for you to want me too."

"I do," he replied, kissing her again.

The movie was coming to an end, so Lo texted Mack to come get him. When they walked outside, Mack was waiting just like he said he would be. Lo gave Janet a kiss then got in the car.

"Who's the new girl?" Mack asked as he pulled off.

"Janet. She goes to my school. I'm feeling her, bro. She's different. She's not from the hood, and she's well-mannered and loves family. I'm so into her."

"What happened to Jati?"

"I'm still with her and I have feelings for her, but Janet's just different. She's the opposite of me. Like hot and cold, day and night. No matter what, they go together."

"I feel you, bro. Just follow your heart. You're still young. You have your whole life ahead of you, and there will be plenty of girls to choose from. If you're rocking with Jati, when you go down there, make sure you keep that vest on."

Lo didn't even pay mind to what Mack was saying. He just said. "I know!" His mind was on Janet. Her beautiful face was stuck on his mind.

# TWENTY – ONE

**LO DIDN'T REALIZE HOW SERIOUS THE BEEF WAS WITH HIS** brother and Second Street. As he sat on Jati's front porch, he must have watched Mark and Paco drive by at least twenty times, ice grilling him. Lo wasn't worried; he had his vest on. He thought to himself wondering if it was worth it being there with Jati. Every day he was there, his life was in harm's way, and at any time they could run up on him.

"Lo, are you okay?" Jati asked as she also saw the stare from the enemy.

"Yeah, I'm good. I don't know why they keep driving around staring at me." Lo knew he was across enemy lines. He also knew that if one of those Second Street niggas was on the south side, they'd be dealt with instantly.

"Let's get off the porch and go inside. Nobody's home," Jati said as she got up.

"Damn," Lo said, smacking her on her fat ass.

Jati didn't have to force her ass to move. It did that all by itself. Just the look of it gave Lo an erection. She sat on her sofa and separated her legs, inviting him to a meal, and he dug right in. The vest was uncomfortable and heavy as he lay on her. He got up, unstrapped the vest from each side, and took it off, letting it fall behind the sofa.

"That's better," Jati said.

Lo leaned in and kissed her. She had nice juicy lips that he loved to suck on. He started grinding on her pussy as she moaned with excitement. She unbuckled his pants and released his dick.

"Damn," she said as she caressed it.

Lo knew she wanted him, and he wanted her too. It had been a long time waiting. He unzipped her pants and slid his hand down there, playing with her pussy. She was tight and wet.

"You sure you want to do this?" Lo asked.

Jati said yes in a seductive voice. Lo slid her pants halfway down her legs, just revealing her ass and her pussy that poked out through her panties. He pulled off her panties also.

"Wow," he said, looking at the most beautiful pussy he had ever seen.

No one was home, but he had to be very cautious not to get caught. It was very uncomfortable as he tried to penetrate her walls. His penis didn't want to go in. He was too thick, and her pussy was too tight. Lo felt the warmness of her pussy as he rubbed his head against her.

He aligned the tip of his dick with her wet hole and inserted it slowly. She moaned as he was easing in inch by inch. Then the screen door opened.

~ ~ ~

♫ There's a war going on outside no man is safe from. You can run, but you can't hide forever. ♫

Mobb Deep shot through the subwoofers. Mack was in war mode. He was dressed in all black, with his Kevlar vest on. He pulled into the Gardens and slowly strolled through his projects. Before he parked as he usually did, he circled the hood. He passed the mailboxes, where he noticed his soldiers posted up.

His soldiers locked eyes with him and began to follow him as he got closer. Mack noticed Juice in the crowd. He signaled with his index finger that he was turning around. Juice nodded his head. Mack lowered the music as he hit the center and caught himself thinking about the past year. Business was popping with Rico and his corner. Since he got into a war, he had to put his business with Rico aside.

It was too risky, and he didn't want Rico to get hot because of his noise. Instead of sticking around, Rico took a vacation. Once the beef simmered down, he would reach out to him. He thought about Ricky as he made a U-turn. His eyes got glassy. He knew that if Ricky was around, he would be right on the front line of this war with him knocking niggas off. He shook his head from the thought of his right-hand man out there doing drugs and snitching on his own peoples.

It was about 4:30, mid-July, hot and hazy out. The hood was popping. DJ Omar brought out his DJ equipment and lit up the hood. All the hood chicken heads were out wearing their skimpiest outfits, trying to catch a hood nigga to take care of them.

Juice, Kamikaze, JO, and Junito were posted up at the mailbox, while George, Mar Mar, Drunk Monk, and Chalk stood across the street. Mack had shooters on each side, watching each direction. After he greeted everyone, he pulled Juice to the side.

"How much work we got left?" Mack asked.

"We sitting on a brick and a half, and ten pounds left that we bagged up."

"After that shit is done, we gonna fall back on the shipments. Holla at King, tell him we on vacation until further notice. I spoke to Rico already, he on vacation to until this war cools down. Take your cut. You still got fiends on your phone?"

"Yeah, I'm good bro," Juice said.

As the night dimmed down, the goons and the guns came out. Everyone was ready for war. Mack had three goons posted up on each corner, while him, Junito, and Juice played the mailboxes. If any of them Second Street niggas went up there, they'd be Swiss cheesed. During the summer there were at least three shootouts a week on the south side. Just as you would expect, the shootouts were back on Second Street minutes later.

"Juice, you seen Husky today?" Mack asked.

"Yeah. He was meeting up with Lo to chill with some bitches at the Microtel.

~ ~ ~

"Let me get two rooms, nonsmoking," Husky said to the receptionist.

They were four deep at the Microtel. Lo, Husky, Donny, and their cousin Jo-ski. They each had a separate room with separate ladies.

"It's about to go down," Lo thought to himself as he snatched his room key from Husky, then departed.

When Lo entered the room, he was hit with the ice-cold air from the AC. He turned it down a notch to set the temperature just right. He kicked his shoes off and looked at the oversized mirror that hung behind the King size bed. He smiled and rubbed his hands together. Then there was a soft knock at the door.

There she was looking glamorous in her jean jumper that hugged her body tightly. Lo just smiled as he admired her beautiful frame. Jati smiled back, loving the way he was drooling over her.

"Fix your face. You act like you never seen me before," she smirked.

"Sorry, you just look so beautiful today, and you smell good too."

Jati laughed as she walked in and sat on the bed. Lo could tell that she was nervous. There was no one around, and he had her all to himself.

"What time do you have to go home?" Lo asked.

"I'm with Kelly, so around two."

Lo looked at the clock, and it read 10:30. "Well get comfortable."

Jati plopped off her sneakers and lay on the bed. The jumper was so tight on her that he could see the print of her pussy lips through her pants. He jumped on the bed and got to it. He made the first move and kissed her. They kissed for ten minutes before he got up and turned off the lights. The room was dark, and the scent of her lotion mixed with her body sprays filled the room.

The smell turned him on so much that every time he kissed her, his erection would jump, and he grinded on her. She grinded back, letting out a moan. Lo unclipped the left side of her jumper, then caressed her left breast. It was so soft as he felt her nipple through her shirt and bra. He released his lips from hers and slowly went after her neck like a vampire. Jati was in heaven.

She knew from the first time she saw Lo, that he was the one to deflower her. She was in sixth grade, and he was hanging out with her cousin Dee outside her school, Hickory Manor. She was starstruck as his blue eyes made her melt.

Dee noticed the tension and demanded her to go home. Jati told her best friend Shema that Lo was the man of her dreams. A few years later she was cuddled up in the Microtel with him.

Lo unclipped the other buckle and loosened her jumper. He slowly lifted up her shirt to reveal her navel. He placed the shirt just below her bra. He kissed her flat stomach, and Jati gave off a slight giggle. Lo released his tongue and licked her stomach, slowly moving down. He planted his face between her legs and inhaled her scent. She smelled good. He then moved his face back to hers and kissed her on her swollen lips.

"You ready?" he asked seductively.

Jati didn't say a word. She slowly unbuttoned the sides of her jumper, which held her ass together. Lo removed his jeans. She was sexier with it, taking her time to remove her clothes. He thought she was having a hard time because of how tight it was. Once she removed the jumper, she tossed it to the side. Lo leaned in and kissed her again. Now the only thing that was separating their body parts from being exposed was boxers, panties, and bra.

Jati slid her hand down his boxers and grabbed his

erection. Lo caressed her wet spot and slid a finger inside. She was tight, but he knew that from the first time they were together. It was going to be hard trying to penetrate, but this time there wouldn't be any interruptions. He slid off her panties and kissed the insides of her legs. The bed was wet from her juices flowing all over the place.

Lo slid off his boxers and released his erection. He whispered in her ear. "Put it in."

Jati grabbed his dick and rubbed it on her wet clit. She aligned him with her, the tip of his dick touching her opening. Her pussy clutched the tip, and she clinched. Jati took a deep breath and lifted her ass toward his body. The head of his dick entered her warm hole. She let off a loud moan. Lo didn't move. He let her guide him in.

After a couple of minutes, her juices were all over him. Lo slowly went deeper inside her. He knew that it was really her first time, so he took it slow. This was the first time that he had sex with someone that he truly had feelings for. Jati moaned as she clawed his back. He went even deeper inside her. It felt so good that they both were moaning.

"Ahhhhh, I love you, Lo," she screamed out in pleasure and pain.

"I love you too, baby," he replied.

Her juices were pouring out of her like a fountain. He was digging in her, grinding on her inner walls. She came multiple times but kept going harder and faster until he exploded inside her. They were in pure ecstasy. He lay there, still inside her as she rubbed his sweaty back.

"That was so good." She smiled. "Let's do it again."

# TWENTY – TWO

*Two Months Later*

THE SUMMER BLEW BY FAST. TOMORROW WAS THE START of another school year for Lo. It was his sophomore year. He laid out his crispy fresh outfit and went to take a shower. It was his girlfriend Jati's freshman year, so he had to look fly for her. Once he was done, he sat there thinking about the past three months. The war between the south side and Second Street was turned up. The cookouts and the tournaments in the Hole were live.

He thought about the movies with Janet and when he took Jati's virginity. He smiled at his summer because he would never forget it. He made money and spent it. He wondered what tomorrow would bring as he dozed off to sleep.

"Lo, you ready?" AR asked.

"Yeah, I'm ready. Mello, you ready?"

"Yup! You know it."

"You hear the crowd?" Mello asked Lo as they chanted his name.

"Yeah, bro, they came to you," Logan said, sipping his water.

Lo looked at the mic in his hand and thought for a quick second. He took a sip of water to quench his thirst and placed the mic to his mouth and spoke. "Yeah!"

Mello hopped onstage with AR right behind him. They wore white tees with an *H* ironed on them representing the Hole. The crowd was going crazy as Lo spit his third single off his mixtape. He stepped onstage, and the crowd roared.

After spitting his first song, the beat dropped, and his new single filled the speakers. The song was called "Visions." As he gazed at the crowd, the hook to "Visions" shot through the speakers. He then noticed a Spanish girl with jet-black hair staring at him through the crowd. It was a familiar face, but something seemed different. It was her hair. This time it was straightened. Lo spit his verse intentionally to her. The crowd noticed and pushed her to the front of the crowd. She blushed as he grabbed her hand and rapped his final verse to her. "Meet me at the side of the stage," Lo told her.

He grabbed his water bottle and headed off the stage. There she was, waiting on him. She was the one haunting his dreams. Lo analyzed her from the floor up. She wore caramel brown sandals, a white sundress that fitted nice and tight on her frame, and caramel accessories to match her sandals. Her hair was flat-ironed straight. To his surprise she only wore lip gloss and no makeup. She was even beautiful up close in person. Lo approached her with such a swag that she had to smile. He grabbed her hand.

"My name is Lo. What's yours?"

She sounded like an angel when she spoke. "My name is—"

~ ~ ~

Jati hurried and ran to the bathroom anticipating vomiting. Her mouth was watery, and she was drooling over the toilet holding her stomach. For the past ten minutes, she'd been having this sharp pain in her stomach, and her menstrual flow was heavy. It was or seemed like signs of her period. So she thought. She sat on the toilet cleaning herself with towels.

"Jati, are you okay?" Kelly asked.

"No. I don't know what's wrong with me. I've been throwing up, and now I'm bleeding like crazy," she complained while clutching her stomach. "I gotta use the bathroom."

"Jati, what's wrong with you? Are you pregnant?" Kelly asked, concerned.

She ignored the question as she sat on the toilet in astonishing pain. Liquid was being released from her, and when she looked down, she began to cry. Inside the toilet was blood mixed with other fluids. It'd been almost two months since she had her period. From the look inside the toilet, she knew that she just had a miscarriage. Tears formed in her eyes. Kelly was in disbelief.

"Jati, did you just have a miscarriage?"

"I think so," she said as the tears rolled down her face.

"You gotta tell Lo, and we gotta get you to a hospital."

Jati was speechless. All she could do was cry. She wasn't sure how Lo was going react to her having a miscarriage. Would he leave her? Would he blame her for losing his first child? What would he say? These were just some of the thoughts running through her head as she sat there and continued to cry.

Kelly helped her into the shower, where she just curled up and let the water hit her naked body. After her shower, she got dressed. Before going to the hospital, she dialed Lo's number.

The ringing of his phone woke him up out of the dream he was having. Just when he was about to get the Spanish girl's name. "Damn it," he said, glancing at his phone and noticing that it was Jati. "Hello!"

"Hey, baby, are you asleep?"

"I was. What time is it?"

"It's 11:30. I'm sorry I woke you up. I can't sleep."

"What's wrong?" Lo asked, sensing something was up.

"Umm. Umm." Jati was trying to get the words out. "Umm, I don't know. I'm just missing you," she lied. She didn't know how to tell Lo that she was pregnant and lost the baby. She wasn't even sure if she would ever tell him.

"I miss you too. Are you ready for school tomorrow?"

"Yes!"

"Okay. Well I'ma go back to sleep. I'll see you tomorrow. I love you."

"I love you too," she replied, and the phone went dead.

Lo slammed his fist on the bed upset. He was mad because he didn't get the name of the girl in his dream. He got up and turned off his light, then dozed back off hoping to get back to that dream.

Jati lay on her bed curled up, holding her stomach, while Kelly lay next to her. The doctors told her that she was seven weeks pregnant and she had a miscarriage.

"It's going to be okay, Jati," Kelly said, comforting her.

~ ~ ~

The first day of school was just like every other year. Everyone wore their hottest gear. Lo met up with Jati at the lockers. They exchanged kisses and said that they would meet up at the same spot at three. The day dragged, and Lo was pleased when the bell rang. As he left the classroom, he ran into Janet. She was still as beautiful as ever.

"Hey, Lo, where have you been? I tried to call you after the party. I haven't heard from you since then. I hope that my mom didn't run you off."

Lo smiled. "Run me off? No, Janet. I was a little uncomfortable. I was feeling the tension from your mom, but I have been busy. You know, ripping and running around. But I can call you later today if you want."

"Sure. Call me. I can't wait."

Lo walked off not wanting to keep Jati waiting. When he got to the lockers, she was gone. As he left the school, he saw niggas from the Hole and south side posted up. He chilled with them for a while before heading home.

# TWENTY – THREE

**THE NEXT DAY AFTER SCHOOL LO DECIDED TO GO PICK UP** some new sneakers for him and his girl. As he got to the steps, he noticed a few of his old heads posted up. Lo knew that it was strange, but he kept moving forward and watching his back, glancing up and down the street. The war with the other hoods was getting crazy. He saw Juice parked up waiting for his girlfriend to come out. He dapped his homies, then went to greet Juice. He had his music low, and from Lo's point of view, he was sleeping. So he crept up on him as if he was going to lay him down, using his hand like a gun.

"BAM! Caught you slipping," Lo said to Juice.

Juice looked up by surprise. "Nobody killing nothing at a school. Too many witnesses."

Lo laughed as he gave Juice dap. "What's good, cuz, you aight?"

"I'm boo'd, Lo. Did you hear the news?"

"No, what happened?"

"Rob got shot in front of his house."

"What?" Lo asked, surprised. "Who shot him?"

"Some young niggas from Second Street."

"Did he die?"

"Nobody knows anything yet. They just saying that he got shot. So make sure you stay on point and be safe out here. Shit about to get ugly out here."

"Damn, cuz," Lo said, worried about Rob. "Aight, I'ma be cool."

"I hope you still wearing that vest like your brother said," Juice reminded him.

"Don't worry, it's right here," Lo replied, hitting his chest. He just lied to Juice. He forgot to put it on this morning, but he wasn't worried about anything because he was going straight home after he picked up some sneakers. He was going to get with Jati later and wanted to surprise her with a pair of sneakers.

Lo gave Juice dap and walked toward his crew in a state of shock, and everybody knew it.

"Lo, you heard what happened to your cousin Rob?" VS asked.

"Yeah, Juice just told me. I'm fucked up, bro."

"He gonna be aight. Let's go grab those kicks," VS said, patting his pocket.

Lo was confused as to why VS patted his pocket but listened to him as they headed for the bus stop. Lo was quiet in his thoughts as they waited on Hanover Avenue for the bus. The bus arrived, and they got on.

"Rob going to be good, I can feel it," Lo said. VS didn't speak. He went into his pocket and pulled out a .380. "What the fuck you doing with that?"

"Protection. Fuck them Second Street niggas. They don't know me. I'll hit one of them niggas up."

"You had that shit in school?"

"Yeah. I stay strapped."

"VS, you crazy."

Lo felt comfortable that his man was strapped. Even though he didn't play with guns, he was protected. VS and Lo hopped off the bus on Eighth and Hamilton. They walked into parks and were greeted by Kim.

"Kim, where them 13s at?" Lo asked.

"We got them right here Lo. Size seven, right?"

"Yup!"

Lo and his family had been buying sneakers from there his entire life. Kim went to the back and brought out two pair of 13s for him. Lo tried one on, and he loved the way they looked. He couldn't wait to rock them in school.

Kim placed the two boxes in a bag as Lo handed her $240. He grabbed the bag and left the store with VS trailing behind him. He didn't want anything. They waited at the bus stop for the bus to take them back to the east side.

It was about 4:50 when Lo arrived home. Mack called him soon as he walked in the door to tell him about what happened to Rob.

"I know, bro. Juice told me after school. I'm about to watch the news now," Lo said, turning to the 69 news. He caught it just in time.

"Breaking news: A twenty-eight-year-old man was shot outside his Ridge Avenue home this afternoon. Witnesses say that there was a fight between the victim and an unidentified male. Witnesses then saw a young man walk up behind the victim and shot him in the head. The victim who police haven't identified yet was transported to Lehigh Valley Hospital Cedar Crest, where he was pronounced dead. We will update you more at six. This is

Jackie Frost at 69 news."

Lo couldn't believe that his cousin had died. He thought that he was going to be okay. He still had Mack on the phone as he headed back out to meet up with Jati.

"Are you good, lil bro?" Mack asked.

"Not really, but I will be okay. I'm going to meet Jati now. Then we're coming back to the crib for a while."

"You wearing that vest right?"

"Yeah," he lied again. Knowing that he should have it on, Lo turned around to go get it. As he was walking, a black van pulled beside him. The side door opened up. Before he could do anything, shots rang out.

POP! POP! POP!

Mack heard the shots and his little brother's phone hit the ground. "Lo? Lo?" he yelled through the phone.

*To order books, please fill out the order form below:*
*To order films please go to www.good2gofilms.com*

Name:_____

Address:_____

City:_____ State:_____ Zip Code:_____

Phone:_____

Email:_____

Method of Payment:     Check     VISA  MASTERCARD

Credit Card#:_____

Name as it appears on card: _____

Signature: _____

| Item Name | Price | Qty | Amount |
|---|---|---|---|
| 48 Hours to Die – Silk White | $14.99 | | |
| A Hustler's Dream - Ernest Morris | $14.99 | | |
| A Hustler's Dream 2 - Ernest Morris | $14.99 | | |
| A Thug's Devotion – J. L. Rose and J. M. McMillon | $14.99 | | |
| All Eyes on Tommy Gunz – Warren Holloway | $14.99 | | |
| Black Reign – Ernest Morris | $14.99 | | |
| Bloody Mayhem Down South – Trayvon Jackson | $14.99 | | |
| Bloody Mayhem Down South 2 – Trayvon Jackson | $14.99 | | |
| Business Is Business – Silk White | $14.99 | | |
| Business Is Business 2 – Silk White | $14.99 | | |
| Business Is Business 3 – Silk White | $14.99 | | |
| Cash In Cash Out – Assa Raymond Baker | $14.99 | | |
| Cash In Cash Out 2 - Assa Raymond Baker | $14.99 | | |
| Childhood Sweethearts – Jacob Spears | $14.99 | | |
| Childhood Sweethearts 2 – Jacob Spears | $14.99 | | |
| Childhood Sweethearts 3 - Jacob Spears | $14.99 | | |
| Childhood Sweethearts 4 - Jacob Spears | $14.99 | | |
| Connected To The Plug – Dwan Marquis Williams | $14.99 | | |
| Connected To The Plug 2 – Dwan Marquis Williams | $14.99 | | |
| Connected To The Plug 3 – Dwan Williams | $14.99 | | |
| Cost of Betrayal – W.C. Holloway | $14.99 | | |
| Cost of Betrayal 2 – W.C. Holloway | $14.99 | | |
| Deadly Reunion – Ernest Morris | $14.99 | | |
| Death by Association – Ernest Morris | $14.99 | | |
| Death by Association 2 – Ernest Morris | $14.99 | | |
| Dream's Life – Assa Raymond Baker | $14.99 | | |
| Flipping Numbers – Ernest Morris | $14.99 | | |

| | | | |
|---|---|---|---|
| Flipping Numbers 2 – Ernest Morris | $14.99 | | |
| He Loves Me, He Loves You Not - Mychea | $14.99 | | |
| He Loves Me, He Loves You Not 2 - Mychea | $14.99 | | |
| He Loves Me, He Loves You Not 3 - Mychea | $14.99 | | |
| He Loves Me, He Loves You Not 4 – Mychea | $14.99 | | |
| He Loves Me, He Loves You Not 5 – Mychea | $14.99 | | |
| Killing Signs – Ernest Morris | $14.99 | | |
| Killing Signs 2 – Ernest Morris | $14.99 | | |
| Kings of the Block – Dwan Willams | $14.99 | | |
| Kings of the Block 2 – Dwan Willams | $14.99 | | |
| Lord of My Land – Jay Morrison | $14.99 | | |
| Lost and Turned Out – Ernest Morris | $14.99 | | |
| Love & Dedication – W.C. Holloway | $14.99 | | |
| Love Hates Violence – De'Wayne Maris | $14.99 | | |
| Love Hates Violence 2 – De'Wayne Maris | $14.99 | | |
| Love Hates Violence 3 – De'Wayne Maris | $14.99 | | |
| Love Hates Violence 4 – De'Wayne Maris | $14.99 | | |
| Married To Da Streets – Silk White | $14.99 | | |
| M.E.R.C. - Make Every Rep Count Health and Fitness | $14.99 | | |
| Mercenary In Love – J.L. Rose & J.L. Turner | $14.99 | | |
| Money Make Me Cum – Ernest Morris | $14.99 | | |
| My Besties – Asia Hill | $14.99 | | |
| My Besties 2 – Asia Hill | $14.99 | | |
| My Besties 3 – Asia Hill | $14.99 | | |
| My Besties 4 – Asia Hill | $14.99 | | |
| My Boyfriend's Wife - Mychea | $14.99 | | |
| My Boyfriend's Wife 2 – Mychea | $14.99 | | |
| My Brothers Envy – J. L. Rose | $14.99 | | |
| My Brothers Envy 2 – J. L. Rose | $14.99 | | |
| Naughty Housewives – Ernest Morris | $14.99 | | |
| Naughty Housewives 2 – Ernest Morris | $14.99 | | |
| Naughty Housewives 3 – Ernest Morris | $14.99 | | |
| Naughty Housewives 4 – Ernest Morris | $14.99 | | |
| Never Be The Same – Silk White | $14.99 | | |
| Scarred Knuckles – Assa Raymond Baker | $14.99 | | |

| | | | |
|---|---|---|---|
| Scarred Knuckles 2 – Assa Raymond Baker | $14.99 | | |
| Shades of Revenge – Assa Raymond Baker | $14.99 | | |
| Slumped – Jason Brent | $14.99 | | |
| Someone's Gonna Get It – Mychea | $14.99 | | |
| Stranded – Silk White | $14.99 | | |
| Supreme & Justice – Ernest Morris | $14.99 | | |
| Supreme & Justice 2 – Ernest Morris | $14.99 | | |
| Supreme & Justice 3 – Ernest Morris | $14.99 | | |
| Tears of a Hustler - Silk White | $14.99 | | |
| Tears of a Hustler 2 - Silk White | $14.99 | | |
| Tears of a Hustler 3 - Silk White | $14.99 | | |
| Tears of a Hustler 4- Silk White | $14.99 | | |
| Tears of a Hustler 5 – Silk White | $14.99 | | |
| Tears of a Hustler 6 – Silk White | $14.99 | | |
| The Last Love Letter – Warren Holloway | $14.99 | | |
| The Last Love Letter 2 – Warren Holloway | $14.99 | | |
| The Panty Ripper - Reality Way | $14.99 | | |
| The Panty Ripper 3 – Reality Way | $14.99 | | |
| The Solution – Jay Morrison | $14.99 | | |
| The Teflon Queen – Silk White | $14.99 | | |
| The Teflon Queen 2 – Silk White | $14.99 | | |
| The Teflon Queen 3 – Silk White | $14.99 | | |
| The Teflon Queen 4 – Silk White | $14.99 | | |
| The Teflon Queen 5 – Silk White | $14.99 | | |
| The Teflon Queen 6 - Silk White | $14.99 | | |
| The Vacation – Silk White | $14.99 | | |
| Tied To A Boss - J.L. Rose | $14.99 | | |
| Tied To A Boss 2 - J.L. Rose | $14.99 | | |
| Tied To A Boss 3 - J.L. Rose | $14.99 | | |
| Tied To A Boss 4 - J.L. Rose | $14.99 | | |
| Tied To A Boss 5 - J.L. Rose | $14.99 | | |
| Time Is Money - Silk White | $14.99 | | |
| Tomorrow's Not Promised – Robert Torres | $14.99 | | |
| Tomorrow's Not Promised 2 – Robert Torres | $14.99 | | |
| Two Mask One Heart – Jacob Spears and Trayvon Jackson | $14.99 | | |
| Two Mask One Heart 2 – Jacob Spears and Trayvon Jackson | $14.99 | | |

| | | | |
|---|---|---|---|
| Two Mask One Heart 3 – Jacob Spears and Trayvon Jackson | $14.99 | | |
| Wrong Place Wrong Time – Silk White | $14.99 | | |
| Young Goonz – Reality Way | $14.99 | | |
| | | | |
| Subtotal: | | | |
| Tax: | | | |
| Shipping (Free) U.S. Media Mail: | | | |
| Total: | | | |

**Make Checks Payable To: Good2Go Publishing, 7311 W Glass Lane, Laveen, AZ 85339**